GHETTO GAMES

The ghetto games continue in the deadliest games ever played; a bloody game of revenge!

By: G. Prince
"Devoted to Lacing you"

G. Prince
Ghetto Theory Publishing
2014

www.ghettotheorywriting@yahoo.com

Disclaimer

This is a work of absolute fiction! The author has invented and created all of the characters, dialog, and incident, which is purely a product of the author's imagination.

Any resemblance to any actual person's life, or lifestyle; living or dead is purely coincidental, and is not to be associated with the author's imagination, or creative thoughts and expression.

Synopsis

Revenge is the definition of Ghetto Games, as the three young rawest West Coast kingpins, find themselves fighting a deadly battle against the worse enemies that they could ever want to face... Some scandalous, crooked ass cops from the L.A.P.D.

This is part three from the coldest West Coast gangsta tale ever told; Ghetto Games." A guaranteed page turner that is street certified and gangsta approved. The sequel continues!

Table of Content

Chapter 1

A Bullet Got No Love

It was December 23, 1990 and Julian, G-Fly, and Ty was on top of their game. They had 40% of the drugs that came into the Los Angeles area on lock, and they were making a two million dollar profit every week just in there drug empire. The whole crew was eating good, and everyone was devoted to the cause and the family to the fullest. Princess, Tish, Dee Dee, and Gwen ran the drug empire. They were considered the boss bitches that provided the supply and demand. And if you wasn't buying 25 kilos or better, then you wasn't dealing with them. They only dealt with the clientele that they've been dealing with from the beginning. No new people or faces at all. And like clock work, everything ran smoothly. Lady G oversees the escort services, and is the executive secretary and the treasury secretary over all of the business ventures that the youngsters and the woman in the escort service invest in. Every woman who works in the escort service has partner up to start some sort of business, or they start a business venture on their own with the youngster's support. So business was good and Lady G had her hands full dealing with all of the specifics. Nevertheless, she was considered the bottom lady, so that made her queen bitch and she earned her title and position like a 'down and true ride or die bitch. ' She helped Game build the escort service and drug empire from scratch, and once Game died and left his empire to the youngsters, then G-Fly accepted her as his bottom lady and she honor her position with pride. G-Fly became her soul mate and gave her the son that Game couldn't ever give her. And little G was her pride and joy, he just turned 3 years old and is as smart as a whip, and twice as bad and spoiled as any child could ever be. Lady G stirred her rice as she was standing over the stove, and smiled at the thought as she rubs her pregnant belly and thought about how happy little G was gonna be with a little brother. Lady G was 6 months pregnant and happy to be in love and finally have a real family. As a ex-hoe, she thought that she will never be blessed with kids, especially because her first love Game couldn't produce, but now things has change and it feels like all of her dreams was coming true.

G-Fly and Ty was at their dinning room table having a meeting. Julian was in Las Vegas with little Tish laundering the 20 million dollars that they already had profited and had to the side ready to be placed in their off-shore accounts.

Their attorney Ron Johnson accountant who be laundering the money for them, like to meet in Las Vegas because that's where his connection is located at, and considering that the youngsters had a lot of money that they laundered at once, saves John the accounted, the problem of being responsible of transporting the money from point A to point B.

The phone rung as G-Fly and Ty sat at the table enjoying their morning joint.

"Hello," G-Fly said as he answered the phone.

"What's up playa, I see that you're up bright and early this morning." Julian said as he made a brief laugh.

"You damn right I'm up early, why you didn't call us last night?" G-Fly said in a pissed off voice tone.

"Oh, my bad! as soon as me and Tish arrived, it was all business. John was waiting and set up so we went right to work. We didn't finish the class (meaning counting the money), until around 5 o'clock this morning, so after eating breakfast and taking a shower, I figured that you guys should be up by now, so I'm calling to let you know that it's all good."

"Good, now maybe I can get some rest." G-Fly joked.

"Listen, me and Tish is going to do some shopping and a little gambling while we're here, so we'll be back probably Sunday."

"Cool, but remember.... if you hit big, then cash out and enjoy it, but if you loose, then don't chase, because Vegas will break you're ass." G-Fly said as he looked at Ty and laughed as Ty shook his head in agreement and little G ran in the room and jumped on G-Fly lap.

"O'kay playa, if you need me then page me."

"Gotcha, get money!"

"Always." (click)

G-Fly hung up the phone and looked over at Ty and said, "Everything went smooth, and J. and Tish is gonna stay there for the weekend and do some shopping and gambling."

"Cool..! I'ma go take a shower then go pick up the money from the businesses and take it to the bank. What you gonna do today?" Ty asked as he made a funny face at little G and they all laughed.

"Well, I'ma probably take Lady G and my little man here, to Sea World so he can see the big fishes."

"Ooowow daddy, like the ones in my fish tank?" Little G asked.

"Bigger!" G-Fly said as he eyes got big.

"Bigger then Blacky and Red?" little G was referring to his Oscar and Red Devil fish.

"Yep, super, super big." G-Fly said as Ty shook his head in agreement as he rubbed little G's curly hair then gently slapped little G's big head and smiled and walked out.

"Daddy what did you buy mommy for Christmas?"

"Why you ask...! Did your mom tell you to ask me that?"

"Well daddy, you told me to never lie to you, but you also said, to never tell on nobody, so I don't know what to say!" Little G said as he looked up at G-Fly with his big eyes.

G-Fly laughed and said, "O'kay, can you keep a secret?" Little G shook his head yes.

"Now if I tell you, then you can't tell no one."

"O'kay, but not even mommy?"

"Nope, not even mommy!"

"O'kay, but I don't know how I'm gonna get the puppy now!"

G-Fly laughed and said, "I brought her a big house in Brazil."

"What's Brazil?"

"It's a real beautiful county overseas that a lot of blacks go there when they want to live like kings and queens."

"We're gonna live in Brazil?"

"It will be a place where we can go to get away and have fun...you'll love it. Now let's go get some breakfast." G-Fly said as he stood up with little G in his arms and grab the remote control to the TV and cut the TV off as he walked out of the dinning room.

G-Fly walked out of the dinning room carrying his little son as he heard a loud crash from the front door and he walked toward the noise and heard the police say, "DEA get down, get your ass down on the ground... he got a gun, he got a gun," and the police opened fired on G-Fly as G-Fly tried to dive on the ground and shield little G from the bullets.

Lady G heard the loud bang then the police yelling as she made her way toward the front door, then seen the police open fire on her man as he held their baby in his arms. She yelled, "Noooo!" But it was too late.

When the bullets stop Lady G ran over toward G-Fly and little G who was laying in a puddle of blood, and a big police officer grabber her as she was running and flipped her in the air and slammed her on the hard marble floor, and then jumped on her back and tried to handcuff her as she tried to struggle to get free. Then two more police ran over and jumped on her head and back as the first police handcuffed her. Then all they heard was gun fire as one of the police who was on Lady G's back got knocked off of her by a gun shot, and another police who was standing over G-Fly with his gun drawn got hit multiple times and hit the ground shaking to his death. Lady G glanced up in a daze and seen Ty holding two 45 automatics, one in each hand and fired coming out of the barrels of the guns. Their eyes meet for a brief second as Ty gave a gentle smile, and bullets hit his slim body from all directions, as his frame shook from the impact of the bullets and he fell back against the up stair wall, and fell dead to the floor. Lady G closed her eyes real tight as a sharp pain went through her body and her body tensed up and blood started leaking from her vagina. Cindy was in the doorway and yelled, "Get off of her she's pregnant."

The police looked up and turned their guns on Cindy and yelled, "Get the fuck down now!"

Cindy complied as she said, "What have you done? Why have you done this?"

The big white cop ran up on Cindy and handcuffed her then hit her in the back of the head with the butt of his gun, knocking Cindy unconscious. "Go check the damn house!" The big police yelled.

And all of the police except two, left to go search the rest of the house for guns, dope, money, or anybody else. "Joe," one of the other police who stayed back called out to his partner, the big police, "this muthafucka didn't have no gun, he got a TV remote control in his hand, not a fuckin gun!"

The big police walked over and looked at G-Fly hand and seen the TV remote and said, "Damn, I thought you said that he had a gun?" The white police Joe said, to Gust the other police who was standing there next to Fred, Joe's partner.

"When we came in, I thought that he had a gun in his hand.... it looked like a gun!" Gust said in his defense.

"You stupid bastard!" Joe said as he reached down in his ankle holster and pulled out a throw away 3.08 revolver and wiped it off and placed it in G-Fly's hand, then took the TV remote and put it on the table.

Two other polices came from down stairs and one was carrying an Ak-47 and a Mac 10, and the other one said, "It's a big safe in the master bedroom and a smaller one in the other bedroom."

Joe heard sirens coming and said, "Fred call it in and request an ambulance, tell them that we got two police down and need assistance."

Fred picked up his walkie-talkie and made the call. Gust was kneeled down over Steve the police who Ty shot, and Gust motioned his hand back and forth across his throat displaying that the police was dead. Joe looked at Michael who was kneeled down over the other police and shook his head saying that the police didn't make it.

The local police and paramedics rushed in and Joe held up his badge and went over to talk to the other police that arrived. The paramedics ran from person to person checking for a pulse. "Got one over here!" One paramedic yelled.

"I got a pulse over here too and she's pregnant. I think that she's hemorrhaging. We got to get her to the hospital."

They were putting Lady G on the gurney as a police grabbed one of the paramedics and said, "Fuck her, what about them?" And pointed to the two police officers who was shot up laying in a puddle of blood.

"We can't help them now get your hands off of me so I can do my job." The woman paramedic said in a stern tone.

The police let her go as they race out with Lady G on the gurney. The other paramedic was treating Cindy while she was laying on the floor in handcuffs with a big gash in the back of her head. She looked over at little G twisted on the floor dead and a tear ran down her eyes. A paramedic was over G-Fly checking him out and said, "I got a light pulse over here - I need help."

"I'll be alright baby, go help him! Cindy said to the paramedic who was treating her, as the paramedic shook her head and ran over to where G-Fly was laying. Cindy looked up at Gust and said, "You muthafuckin murderer! I hope you all burn in hell for what you did to these innocent people."

"Get her up out of here.... take her down to the station." Gust said to the other police who just arrived.

"I'll pray that you will go to hell for this, you evil, heartless monster.... you sons of Satan!" Cindy yelled as the two police drug her out.

"I don't know what happened in here Joe, but I expect a full report on my desk in 4 hours, and it better be good!" The Captain yelled as he looked around at all of the dead bodies and shook his head. "And I don't want to hear nobody talking to no reporters, this is a "Class A" investigation. Detective I want to know everything about this family that you can find out. And sit two police officers on each of the persons that was taken to the hospital. Detain them both pending further investigation, and don't let anyone talk to them until we find out what the hell is going on." He glanced over at Officer Joe and Officer Fred and then stormed out.

Fred looked over at Joe, and Joe shook his head as he walked away.

After Cindy was taken to the police station they placed here in a small cell alone and then two hours later took her into and investigation room where she sat handcuffed to a steal table. Two Detectives entered the investigation room and the man began speaking.

"Hello Ms. Washington, I realize that today was a real hard day for you to bare with, but we need to get some answers so we can get to the bottom of what just occurred. Can you help us understand this situation better?

"I want to talk to my attorney!" Cindy uttered.

"Yes, but ma'am, you're not charged with any crime as of yet."

"So, I know my rights and I want to call my attorney now!"

"O'kay ma'am, here," the Detective placed a phone in front of Cindy calling her bluff. Usually a person will say that they want to call their attorney because they know that it's their common right, but very seldom do a person have an attorney to call.

Cindy looked at the phone then at the Detectives that was staring at her, and she picked-up the phone and dialed the number that she was taught to remember by heart. G-Fly use to make her study the number over and over as he quizzed her on it, and when she got it right then he would give her a fifty dollar bill. She enjoyed the game and the extra money, but she never thought that she would really have to use it. The phone rung as her memory reflected back on G-Fly as he use to quiz her, then she reflected back on G-Fly and little G laying on the floor all bloody and her thoughts turned mad again.

"Hello!" A man's voice answered the phone.

"Oh, Mr. Johnson?"

"Yes, who am I speaking with?"

"This is Cindy Washington, I'm the live in housekeeper for Xavier and Bryan."

"Yes Cindy, I know who you are."

Cindy heart relaxed a bit, "I was told to contact you whenever there was a problem."

"Yes, how can I help you Ms. Washington?"

Well the police kicked in the door at our house today and shot everybody. They killed Tyquon and the baby, and Lady G and Xavier was rushed to the hospital. I don't know if they're gonna make it."

"Say no more, where are you?"

"I'm at Rampart sub-station."

"Don't speak to no one... I'll be there to get you in an hour O'kay!"

"O'kay." (click) Cindy hung up the phone. "He told me not to speak to anyone and he's on his way." Cindy said as she looked at the two Detectives.

The Detectives looked at one another with a surprise look, and the male Detective (Mr. Wash) asked Cindy "So what did you say your attorney's name is?"

"His name is Ron Johnson."

"Did you say Ron Johnson ma'am?"

"Yes..!"

The two Detectives stood up and said, "An officer will come and get you and take you back to the holding cell. I'll have him bring you something to eat and drink, and well let you know when your attorney arrives. Both the Detectives turned and walked out. They knew who Attorney Ron Johnson was, and if it's the same Attorney Ron Johnson that they knew, then the shits about to hit the fan.

* * * *

Julian was at the dice table with little Tish and little Tish was on a roll. "Eleven," the house man shouted as little Tish throw the dice.

"That's right baby, hit that ass," Julian shouted as he picked up 10 thousand dollars worth of chips and left the other 10 thousand dollar worth down on the table to win.

"Seven," the house man shouted as little Tish rolled again, and jumped up full of joy as she picked up a stack of chips.

Julian gave her high five and packed up a big stack of chips too and his beeper started vibrating. He reached down and looked at the number and it was Princess emergency code and number. He packed up is cell phone and called the number as Tish hit a six on the dice. "Hello!"

Julian said as he covered up his left ear so he could hear better.

"J, this is P..!"

"What's up baby?"

"Listen, I just got a call from Attorney R. J. and he said that he got a call fro Cindy saying that the main house got ran into by the police, and they killed T, and little G, and Fly and Lady G is in critical condition and it's not looking good. What do you want me to do? Hello, hello?"

"Yeah, I'm here! Listen, call the hospital and see what you can find out... where is Cindy now?"

"R. J. went to go get her from the sub-station, she's at Rampart!"

"O'kay, get her out and call a meeting. I'm on my way back now, so ya'll meet me at the house in South Pasadena and watch your backs.

O'kay baby, see you soon." (click)

Julian looked over at Little Tish who crapped out already and was looking at him as he spoke on the phone. His whole body language changed and she could tell that something was wrong. Julian looked at her and said, "We got to go, 'G-Red'!" Little Tish's eyes got big as they grabbed their chips and left.

Chapter 2
Vengeance is Ours

Two hours later Julian and little Tish pulled up to the safe house in South Pasadena and was met as they got out of the car by Princess and Dee Dee, and both of them had teary eyes as they hugged Julian and little Tish and walked with them back into the house were Big Bro, Little Momma, Cindy and Gwen was patiently waiting with red eyes.

Julian sat down at the table and said, "what happened?"

Princess eyes started to tear up as she said, "they killed Ty and little J, and G-Fly's in critical condition with multiple gun shot wounds to is body, he got shot twelve times and he's in a comma. He might not make it! Lady G is in stable condition now, but she lost the baby. Ron is trying to get the detainer off of her now, and he want's you to call him as soon as you can."

Julian's eyes watered with pain and anger as he dialed Ron cell phone number. "Hello! Yeah this is Julian...! Do they got a case? Then what was they looking for? Who Ty? That's good for their ass! Who was responsible for the raid? Yeah find out! A gun in his hand? That's why they killed an innocent baby? That don't sound right? Yeah keep me posted and call me the minute you hear something. Stay low...what for - I didn't do nothing! O'kay, find out then and let me know something. Alright, later!" Julian hung up the phone and said, "They haven't came up with no charges yet, but he want us to lay low until he finds out what's going on. They're saying that they got a tip that, that house was a safe house where we keep drugs at and when they came in, G-Fly pulled a gun and tried to shield himself with little G so they open fired. Then Ty ran out shooting and killed two officers before they open fired on him and killed him. They didn't find no drugs, just guns, money, and a half a pound of weed. But they only got 96 thousand dollars out of the safes along with some documents regarding our investments corporation which is strictly legit. So the raid was a set up of some kind and we need to find out why? Cindy what did you see?"

"Well when I heard the gun shots I got up because I was laying down, then I heard Lady G yell and more gun shots, so I rush to the doorway and seen gun smoke and bodies everywhere. I seen little G laying in G-Fly's arm like he was trying to shield him from the gun shots, and then I seen the police all on top of Lady G's back and I yelled at them to get off of her because she's pregnant, and they turned their guns on me, and I thought that they were going to kill me. They told me to lay down and i did, and this big police handcuffed me, then hit me in the head with something and it knocked me unconscious. When I woke up, the paramedic was around me and police was everywhere. They treated me and when one of them seen that G-Fly had a pulse, I told the one helping me to go help G-Fly, and they snatch G-Fly up on the gurney and took him out. Then I seen little G laying in a puddle of blood and I went off! I called them murders and they grabbed me and rushed me out of there. When I got to the station they tried to question me, but I knew better to say anything, so I asked to call my attorney and they gave me a call and I called Ron. G-Fly made me remember the number when he use to play that game with me; remember?" Julian smiled and shook his head. "I think after they shot G-Fly and little G, Ty seen it and came out shooting. Because he killed a couple of them before they got him." Cindy said as she shook her head yes.

"Listen this shit is about to get real ugly! And if you chose to participate, then you might not make it out alive. So if you don't want to take this ride, then I understand, you can take your wealth and materialistic gain and leave now and never look back. We will not hold it against you." Julian looked around and nobody budged. "Cindy, I need you to play a special part for us." Cindy stood there with her eyes big and heart racing.

"O'kay, whatever you need me to do."

"I need you to deal with the burial arrangements and the selling of the main house. We don't need that place no more. You'll stay here in this house for the time being, and take care of our more significant business matters. So if one of us goes to jail, then we can contact you to call Ron for us and notify me. We also need you to watch over Lady G until she gets better, because we shouldn't be seen right now until we find out what's going on. They might have a warrant out for us, so we got to stay low until we know what is really going on. Do you understand?"

"Yes...!"

"O'kay, listen, I need you to go up stairs until we finish our meeting, because you don't need to be around this aspect of our thoughts."

"Okay baby, whatever you say!" Cindy said as she walked away.

"Listen, we're gonna find out what police was involved and make him tell us what's going on and why? Then I'ma send him to hell! Ladies, get rid of the rest of the work and secure the money, this might be our last dance with that shit. Princess, make sure that Cindy got as much money as she needs to bury our family right. And, I need you to contact Treasure and let her know that our businesses are being watched, so stay professional. When we find out more, then will move accordingly, until then, stay low and out of sight. Any question? Good, now let's go to work. Big Bro I need you and Little Momma on point, so stay close and keep your eyes open."

"Gotcha."

"O'kay baby, Little Momma uttered as they all hugged and kissed.

* * * *

The Captain of the Los Angeles Rampart district was furious about the undisclosed raid on the youngster mansion. He was showing every bit of his anger as he questioned DEA Officer Joe Adams, Fred Smith, and Gust Jones about their authority and procedure.

"Who's in charge here got-dam-it?" The Captain yelled.

"You are Sir." Officer Lieutenant Joe Adams replied.

"Then why wasn't I informed of this raid that took place by my officers in my district?"

"Sir., like I've mentioned in my report, we got a tip from a reliable source, one of our confidential informers, and as we surveillance the premises we observed suspicious activities so we moved in. Once we gained entrance to the residence a man came at us with a gun using a baby as his shield, and we felt that our live was in jeopardy, so we open fired on the hostile suspect. After we subdued the situation, another suspect came out of no where, and shot officer Ed Brown, and Troy Scott before we was able to take him out."

"Got-dam-it..! I read the report and honestly, I think that it's a bunch of bullshit. It reeks of lies and deceit! I've been in this business for over 30 years and I have not ever seen a display of scandalous, devious, malicious acts played out in an insubordinate way. You officers went totally against protocol and the result of it is, two dead police officers, one dead three year old child, and his father laying in a comma in critical condition, and his mother who was brutally slammed to the ground while she was 6 months pregnant, and as a result, experienced a miscarriage."

"Sir., those are notorious drug dealers, they run at the least 30% of the cocaine that came through Los Angeles!"

"Is that right? So you guys found some drugs at the residence that you raided?"

"No Sir., but we found guns, money, and weed." Officer Adams firmly stated.

"Well officer Adams, I hate to inform you, but they also were well established productive citizen who own a lot of very lucrative business ventures. They are very well off, and have one of the best attorney's in the whole California State. Not only are we facing a multi-million dollar law suit, but the Media is on this story like ants to a dead bug, and the Internal Affairs is on our asses like the Grim Reaper. I'm not gonna even try to cover your asses on this one. You were dead wrong, you went against protocol and common procedures, and you have nothing to show for it but a lot of unjustified dead bodies and unbelievable excuses. Therefore, I'm force to place you all on suspension pending the out come of the Internal Affair investigation. And you better be glad that you're not in handcuffs right now. Now hand over you damn badges and guns. And I advise you to get a good attorney to represent you, because you're going to need one. Now clean out your things and if I see you back around this department, I'll personally have you arrested."

Joe, Fred, and Gust handed over their guns and badges and walked out of the Captain's office into the harden stares of their co-worker. Their actions put the whole department under intense investigation, and every police in the department was mad about it. Especially the fact, that two officers got killed during their kamikaze plot. They went to clean out their desk and locker's and then left. Once in the parking lot, Fred and Gust looked at Joe, and Fred said, "We fucked up big time on this one!"

"Do you think that we'll go to prison on this?" Gust asked.

"I doubt it, because if so, then we wouldn't be walking out of there like this. But we got to make some moves and get some extra money quick, so we can get away when this is all over with. Are you guys still down with me?" Joe asked.

"Yeah Joe, you know I'm down! We've been partners for way to long now to break up." Fred said with a grin.

"I guess so," Gust said. I don't think that it can get no worse then this!" And they all laughed.

"O'kay, I'm gonna contact some people and make some moves, and see what I can come up with for us. Stay ready and stick with the story!"

"O'kay."

"Gotcha."

They all shook hands and departed.

* * * *

Joe called his friend from the Bay Area who be putting him up on robberies and big time drug dealers, the same friend who put Joe up on the youngsters and there illegal empire. Joe knew that his long time friend and informant has always been reliable, and every time Joe and his police crew would go rob a drug dealer, or pull a raid on a drug dealer place, then Joe would give his Bay Area friend the dope to sell for them for a whole-sale price.

Joe walks into the pool hall and is searched by the security, then escorted into his friend's office.

"Joe my old friend, damn you guys really made a mess of things on the last job, didn't you?"

"Cut the crap Carl..! That wasn't a good job, those muthafuckas didn't have a room full of drugs or guns. You sent us on a bad job and you know it!"

"Joe come on man, have I ever sent you on a bad job? Them young muthafuckas is kingpins, that's Games young protégés, and that pregnant bitch is Games old bottom hoe. When he died he left everything to them.

They're just half ass legit now, so if you don't catch them slippin' right, then it's a waste of time!"

"I wish that you would have told me this shit before. I lost my fuckin job behind this shit, and also two good friends. And they're threatening to bring me and my crew up on charges. So my ass is in a sling! I need a couple of good licks now, so I can get some extra money in case I got to get out of the fucking county."

"Don't worry Joe, I got your back! I got a couple of licks for you as we speak, and it should fatten our pockets real good, if you know what I mean. But I warn you, they are heavily armed and it might get ugly, so you can't go in playing."

"Hell, what I got to lose? I already got one foot in hell, and the other in the fuckin' pen!"

"Hey, don't you fuckin' dare try to blame me for your little mishap. You know the consequences of your deeds and actions. You want licks, then I'll give them to you for a cut, you fuck up, then it's your own muthafuckin' fault!"

"I'm not blaming you, I'm just pissed off that it went down like it did." Joe mumbled.

"I understand, and I sympathize with you! But, certain things in life we can't control. You chose this path, now you got to walk it out. No telling, it might lead to better and more prosperous days."

"Or it might lead to hell..!" Joe finished Carl's thoughts then shook his head.

"No telling! But anyway, here is the $240,000 thousand dollars that I owe you from the last batch of drugs that you brung me, and here is the first address on the next lick. They are Mexicans, but the real rowdy type, so stay on your toes." Carl warned.

"Good looking out buddy, I owe you one." Joe said as he got up shook Carl's hand and left out with a duffle bag full of money.

"Boss, do you want me to send the boys to go get that money back off of him for you?" Carl's big right hand man Big Ghost asked.

"Naw, I'm not finish with him yet! But send some of the boys down to Los Angeles to set up shop. It's time to take over Game's empire. Them youngsters is practically exterminated! One's dead, the other one is in a comma, that crazy bitch is probably in a insane asylum, she lost her man and two children in one day, that got to be hard to bare. And that other young nigga ain't cut like that to run a multi-million dollar drug operation on his own. So it's over for them!" Carl and Big Ghost laughed together.

"You're brilliant for setting that move up. You single handedly took down one of the biggest drug empire on the West Coast, and you didn't even have to bust your guns." Ghost said as they laughed at the thought.

"Yep, that's called killing two birds with one stone. Now that punk ass police will get killed or end up in prison, and the rest of Game's empire would either die off, fold, or be copping from us in a minute. Cause we're about to take over the West Coast."

"That's right, I'll toast to that!" And they both hit their glasses together and downed a shot of cognac.

* * * *

"Hello Doctor, you must be new around here?" The cute young black nurse asked.

"Yes, I'm an O. B. GYN specialist and I'm here to see a Ms. Toni Davis."

"Oh yes she's in room 8, she had a very tragic accident. Here's her folder. Do you need any assistance?"

"No Ms., I think that I can handle it. Is there always police guards sitting at her door?"

"Yes Doctor, but you can go right in. Officer James, this is the specialist! He's fine."

"Thank you nurse, remind me to buy you lunch." The doctor flirted and walked into room 8 where his patient was waiting. "Hello Ms. Davis."

Lady G didn't bother to look up, she was morning her lost and her mind was stuck on replay. "Is that anyway to treat your god brother."

Lady G recognized the voice and looked up in shock as she seen Julian dressed in a nice suit and tie with a doctor smock on and a pair of gold frame glasses. "Hi J., what took you so long?" And she gave him a smile.

"I apologize beautiful, they got this place swarming with pigs, and I don't know what's going on yet, so we got to play it from a distance. How you feel?"

"I'm doing much better, I lost my babies! And a tear ran down her eyes as Julian hugged her tight."

"I know baby, I know!"

"They killed G-Fly and little G in cold blood and they gunned down Ty! Ty seen them kill G-fly and little G and how they were jumping on me, and he came out shooting. He killed a couple of them before they got him." Lady G explained.

"I know baby, I heard! We got Cindy out from the sub-station and we are working on getting you out too, so stay strong. Also, G-Fly's not dead yet! He's in a comma and fighting for his life." Lady G's eyes got big. "Yes, we're preparing for a quick transfer, but we got to buy time so we can have the proper equipment to move with. Here!" And Julian gave her a handcuff key. "Give us a couple of days to get things together, and if Ron can't get you free, then we'll come and get you, so play sick until that time O'kay!"

"O'kay, and Julian!" Julian turned and looked at her big pretty red and brown eyes. "Don't let them get away with doing this to us."

"You know better then that, it's G-Red time." And they both smiled. Get some rest baby, you know that we need you strong and healthy."

"O'kay, and Julian!" Julian glanced at Lady G, "Hurry up...!"

"O'kay Sis!" Julian kissed her on the head and left out.

"Excuse me Doctor," the cute nurse waved Julian down.

"Yes?"

"Here's my number if you want to call me."

"Yes I do, and I will." Julian gave her his player smile and walked into the elevator.

G-Fly was on the 10th floor and Julian knew that it was risky, but had to try. He seen the two police sitting outside of a door, so he figure that, that was where G-Fly was being held. Julian walked up looked at the medical chart, and walked in the room without getting a second look from the police outside the door. When he looked at G-Fly his heart skipped a beat. G-Fly had tubes running all up in him and was hooked up to a life support machine. Julian immediately took out his camera and started taking photos of G-Fly and the machine. Then kissed G-Fly on the forehead and said, "Vengeance is ours." Then turned and walked out undetected.

Chapter 3

When A Gangsta' Cries

Julian drove around the block twice to see if he noticed any suspicious vehicles, people, or activities. Once he was sure that everything was clear, he pulled up to mansion and went in. As he entered the front door he seen yellow caution tape circling the crime scene and traces of blood and white tape that outline where the dead bodies were. He seen the little one in the middle of the floor and is eyes watered as his anger flared-up. He ran up the stairs and seen blood and bullet holes on the back wall and the tape outline where Ty body once laid. Julian couldn't hold back the tears as he leaned on the rail next to his God brother's crime scene. He shook his head and wiped his tears on the sleeve of his Versace shut. Then a thought flashed through his mind and he ran into the main study room and pushed a button that was hidden at the bottom of the book shelf and the book shelf unlocked revealing a hidden room where they keep their main safe and where G-Fly put the surveillance equipment that hide the cameras that G-Fly had place all through the house as well as outside the house. Julian laughed at the thought because he tried to argue against having the cameras set up though the room of the mansion, but he was voted out when Ty sided with G-Fly to have it done. They called it their kick-it room, a place where they got high and watch everybody else run around the house not knowing that they were being watched. Julian rewound a couple tapes and seen how the police gained entrance into the house. The house has trick infra-red lights set up, so if a person triggers the sensor, then the cameras would automatically start taping. Julian looked on as he seen the whole incident start playing out before his eyes. "Damn!" Julian uttered as he seen the police open fire on G-Fly and little G. "Bitch ass muthafuckas." Julian whispered as his rage started to boil. Then he seen Lady G run toward G-Fly and little G and get grabbed and slammed to the ground real hard, and the big police jumped on her back real hard then tried to handcuff her as she struggled to get free, then two more police jumped on her back and head as the big police handcuffed her. Then out of no where, Ty comes out with two 45 automatic bussin' like a gangsta' as he shot the police who was standing over G-Fly and little G, and you can see the police body dance as the bullets ripped through him. "That's right my nigga, that's right.... kill his ass!" Julian yelled at the screen. Then Ty shot the police who was on Lady G's head and hit him six times as the bullets knock him clean up off Lady G. "That's right my nigga go hard, kill all of them muthafuckas." Julian yelled as he seen Ty put in work. Then he seen all the police open fired on Ty, and Ty smiled as the bullets hit him multiple times and knocked him back against the back wall as he layed against the wall drenched in his blood with a light grin on his face. "Damn my nigga! Don't trip my nigga, vengeance is ours.... I promise you that!" Julian was in a daze then he seen Cindy yelling from the door way and the big police went over and grappled her down, and hit her in the head with his gun, "Scandalous dirty muthafuckas." Julian mumbled. Then he seen the police call the big police, and the big police walked over to were G-Fly was laying and reached down and grabbed a TV remote control out of G-Fly's hand, and then grabbed a gun from his ankle holster and wiped it off and place it in G-Fly's hand. "Ain't this a Bitch..! They thought G-Fly had a gun, but it was only a damn remote control..! Scandalous muthafuckas realize that they fucked up, so they planted a gun in my niggas hand." Julian pondered the incident then rewind the tape and made a copy of the beginning to the end of the event when the paramedics rush G-Fly out. Julian opened the big safe and stared packing up all the money and documents that was in it. It was at least 1.3 million in the big safe, and all of their Corporations, and business paperwork, and a few bank account statements. He opened the gun case and filled another big suit case full of guns ammo, and silencers. Then went up stairs and grab some clothes, then called Princess on his cell phone. "Hey Ms. P, check it out,. call a meeting I'll be there in an hour." Julian hung up his cell phone and said, "Let the games begin!" Then grabbed the suit cases and left out.

* * * *

"Listen boys, that's the apartment right there." Joe pointed at the old big white two story six unit apartment complex that was across the street. Now five is the apartment where the Mexicans hang out at, but apartment six is where I believe they keep all of the money at. So we got to hit them both but we got to hit them hard, silent, and quick, then get on! Don't underestimate them and don't hesitate to shoot. We can't explain this, and if we fuck up, then our ass is really cooked. So play for keeps! Do ya'll understand?"

"Let's do it!" Gust said.

"You know that I'm down!" Fred said as he screwed his silencer onto the barrel of his gun.

"O'kay let's go." Joe said as they exist the black Bronco truck dressed in orange jump suits with Gas Company written on the back. It was dawn and the sun was at it's lowest of the day. When they entered the up stairs landing, they all put on their ski masks and pulled their guns out. Joe held up two fingers and pointed at Fred and Gust and at apartment five's door. Fred shook his head and put the crow bar into the crack of the door as Gus stood on the other side and Joe was posted at apartment six. Gust counted with his finger, and on three he kicked in the door as Fred used the force of the crow bar by the big lock to bust the door open, and at the same time Joe kicked in apartment six door. "Police, police, get down muthafucka!" Gust yelled as the fat Mexican sitting at the table with two of his crew members reached for his gun that was on the table, and Gust shot him right between the eyes and he feel out of the chair dead before he hit the ground. The other two Mexicans that was at the table dove on the ground with their arms stretched out. Fred ran through the two bedrooms with gun drawn and nobody else was in either one. So he ran back out to where Gus was and started putting straps on the two Mexicans that was on the floor. After he finish he looked at Gust and said, "Go help J."

"Gust shook his head and ran out. As he got to apartment six he yelled "Sights!" And Joe said, "Clear."

Gust came in with his gun drawn. Gust seen Joe had a Mexican man and his wife and 5 year old son laid out on the rug." Watch them as I check the rooms." Joe said as he looked at Gust and Gust shook his head compliance.

Joe went through both rooms with his gun drawn and nobody was present, but he looked in a closet and seen a big safe and grabbed a big suit case and opened it, and seen cocaine stacked neatly through it. "Bingo," Joe said to himself as he grabbed the suit case and the AR-15 rifle that was leaning on the closet wall. He carried the stuff out to the living room where Gust had everyone tied up with plastic straps. Even the little boy was tied up. Joe laughed at the sight and said, "What's the combination to the safe?"

"I don't know, I don't live here amigo." The Mexican said in broken English.

Joe put the gun to the little boy's head and said, "Do you know now puto?"

"O'kay, o'kay, amigo, it's 3, 12, 36!" Joe smiled and went back into the room and opened the safe. Once he opened it he smiled at the stacks of money, and then went to grab both pillow cases and put the money in them, then glanced around the room once again before he walked out.

When he walked in the living room he looked at Gust and said, "take the suit case and go check the other apartment. I'll wait for ya'll to finish so we can go together."

"Gotcha," Gust said as he grabbed the suit case full of dope and went next door where Fred was patiently waiting. Fred already had the money that the Mexicans was counting back in the big duffle bag. Gust walked in and Fred was standing where he had the vantage point over anyone who entered. Gust smiled and place the suit case by the door and said, "I'll check the room for more." Fred shook his head and went into the room to look for more money and dope. Two minute later he walked out with a Tec 9 and said, "There clean, let's roll." And they picked up the black duffle bag and suit case and stepped in the hallway where Joe seen them come out, and shut the apartment door as he walked out to meet them and they all existed out of the building quickly into the light of darkness with their masks still down and guns still exposed. They jumped in the black Bronco and punched out, as they caught a couple of glances from some people who seen them come out with their ski masks on and guns drawn. The Bronco sped away from the curve and was gone as it hit the corner. They hit two blocks and Fred jumped out and put the license plates back on the Bronco, then they drove off again but at a moderate pace.

"We did it! We got them bean eatin' muthafuckas good." Gust said.

"How much do you think we hit for?" Fred asked.

"Well at least 2 to 3 hundred thousand cash and probably 30 kilos of cocaine," Joe said.

"Shit I got at least a hundred thousand from the other apartment so we came up pretty good." Fred said with excitement.

"We sure did partner, we sure did! Now we got a little room to breathe. " Joe uttered with a grin as he got off the freeway and headed for the motel room that they rented.

* * * *

Julian stood before his loyal crew as they all gathered in the big family room of the safe house that was in South Pasadena. He glance at Big Bro, Cindy, and Little Momma who sat on one end, then at Princess , Dee Dee, Gwen, and little Tish who sat at the other. "Listen, what you are about to see will change your life forever. I only hope that you will not let it destroy your spirit and take over your mind." Everyone looked around at one another as Julian pushed play on the VCR. The screen light up and a picture of the police entering into the main mansion played out. Julian sat back in his leather lazy boy chair observing every bodies facial expression and body language, and he could tell that everyone was getting riled up and tempers was flaring with every tear that drop. Ty's big day view caused a up roar, and then a stun silence as everyone witnessed his demise.

"I'ma kill all of them muthafuckas I promise!" Little Tish voiced her pain as her eyes couldn't hold back the tears. Princess hugged her, as they stared lost onto the TV screen.

They seen how the police did Cindy and then everybody jumped up hollering and cursing as they seen the police remove the TV remote from G-Fly's hand and place the gun in it's place.

"Them dirty muthafuckas, there dead!" Big Bro uttered.

"It's on now!" Little Momma said as she stood up and paced the floor back and forth in a rage.

Julian pulse on the TV as the paramedic was carrying Lady G out. "O'kay, now that I got your full attention! There's a lot to be considered here. Now, if we expose the tape, then the police would get arrested and probably place in prison and we'll sue the police department and the State. But, the way that I see it is, that we deal with our own family issues, cause money is not an issue here." And everyone started clapping and agreeing.

"So I want to provide our Attorney with the tape in case of an emergency. But we'll let him know that we don't want him to expose it until the time is right, and about that time we would have either killed our enemies already, be stuck in jail for doing so, dead, or on the run. If we're in jail fighting a case or on the run, then the tape can help our situation a bit, if we're dead, then the truth gets exposed and they still loose, and if we succeed in our intentions, then we will always have a hole card. Now do anyone disagree with this plan?" Julian looked around the room and no one objected. "Good.." Now we got a face to go with the names and Big Bro has some good news that he wants to share, but first I want to asked Cindy if she'll excuse us and go fix us a little snack.

"O'kay baby, I feel you." Cindy said as she got up and kissed Julian on the cheek and left the room.

Julian nodded at Big Bro and Big Bro stood up and began speaking. "Well I got some good news! I got my friend at the DMV to see if she can run these names and get me a current address and as luck would have it, Mr. Gust Jones just brought his 16 year old daughter a brand new

Nissan Sentra and used his current address. So we got a trace on him."

"Which one is he?" Tish asked.

Little Momma handed little Tish a news paper article about the shooting and it had all three of the police picture in it, with their name written under their photos. The article says, "They all got suspended pending an investigation, so we better move fast." Little Momma said, as little Tish past the news paper around.

"O'kay, now we got a trace, a name and the faces, now we need a proper plan of attack and some security on our love ones, so this is what I believe we should do, and the best way to go about it." Julian started telling them his plan as they all attentively listened and shook their heads in agreement.

* * * *

Joe, Fred, and Gust finally finished counting the money and it came up to $348,000 thousand dollars and 36 kilos, and they all was ecstatic. This was by far he biggest lick that they ever came up on and they needed it.

"Listen bro, we got to keep that muthafucka Carl in good graces, because he's selling this cocaine for us and putting us up on these licks. So we'll give him 30 thousand dollars cash, and tell him to bring us the regular 10 thousand dollars off of each kilo. That will give us another $120,000 thousand a piece from the cocaine, and he got another lick for us that should set us straight for life. What you say to that?" Joe knew that his boys was going to go with whatever he decided was best, but he felt that he should ask out of respect.

Fred was a 33 year old white boy that was 6' 4" and weighted 250 pounds, but all muscular. He was a work-out fanatic and took steroids to enhance his muscles. He looked like the big wrestler John Cena and just as crazy. He and Joe were partners for 10 years when Fred was a rookie, and as typical of a police relationship, 'birds of a feather tend to flock together.' You know that I'm down for whatever!" Fred said with a smile on his face.

Gust on the other hand was a short heavy set white boy. He stood 5' 8" and weighted 240 pounds; he was built like a tank. He was 40 years old, married with a 16 year old daughter and a 7 year old son. He'd been on the police force for 15 years and knew that he wasn't going to make it to see his pension, so he was all in for whatever. "Let's do what we got to do, and get it over with so we can go on with our lives." Gust said as he stared back at Joe and Fred as they both shook their heads.

Joe was the ring leader and although they all had no problem shedding blood, Joe was by far the coldest one out of the bunch, because he had military training to go with his gun ho tactics. He spent 6 years in the Marine Corps and was part of a special force tactical unit. So when he became a police officer his military training made him able to establish a higher rank in the police force quicker then the average police. He was only 35 years old, but already regarded as a lieutenant over the Drug Enforcement Agency Unit. He was also married with a 6 and a 5 year old son. He knew he had to stash some money away for them in case he ended up in jail, or on the run. "Well it's settled! I'll call ya'll as soon as I get the info on the next lick. Until then, lay low, and stash that money somewhere safe, because no telling how many of those boys in them suits is coming, and a 100 g's in cash is hard to explain. Ha, ha, ha!" Joe joked as they laughed, grabbed their money and dope, and left.

Chapter 4
Games of A Ghetto Child

The two police was sitting by G-Fly's hospital door as the pretty brown skin nurse with the curvy body approached them and said, "excuse me officers, can you please assist me?" There a hostile man in the women's restroom and I think that he might create a problem."

"Well show us where," the short officer said as he and his rookie partner jumped up ready for some action. They have been sitting at the same door for three days doing nothing but flirting with the cute nurses, so they couldn't wait to display their authority.

"Follow me." The nurse said as her big ass swayed at a melody of it's own.

"Damn!" The young black officer said in a low but direct way as the nurse looked back and smiled at the compliment.

When they entered the restroom two female paramedics was inside and a man was sitting on the toilet with his pants down.

"Sir., your in the women's restroom, you need to pull up your pants and come with us!" Then the two police dropped to the ground shaking as the taser sent electric volts through their bodies. Gwen and Dee Dee handcuffed the two policemen as Big Bro pulled up his pants laughed and then took their guns, and duck taped their mouth and legs and put them in the restroom storage closet, "Come on, we got to move fast." Big Bro said as he through on a Doctor smock and they all left out.

As they entered G-Fly's room, little Tish was there with the retired register nurse that they hired to assist them. The nurse was reconnecting G-Fly's life support machine to a little generator and they placed him on a gurney and pushed him out of the room and down into the elevator.

"Excuse me, hold the elevator," the Doctor said as the elevator door closed on her without the other people on it trying to stop it so she could catch a ride." How rude," the doctor said as the elevator door closed before she could reach it.

Princess looked at Gwen and Dee Dee as they were dressed as paramedics, and then at G-Fly as he was covered up and being push by Big Bro as the RN that they hired walked along side of the gurney rolling the life support machine. The elevator opened up and they all hurried up down the corridor and outside to the stolen paramedic ambulance. They put G-Fly in, then Dee Dee, Princess, little Tish, and RN named Joann jump in the back, while

Big Bro and Gwen ran around and jump in the driver and passenger seat and drove off.

Julian walked right by the officer who was posted in front of Lady G's door. Julian was dressed as a Doctor so he didn't draw no suspicion. The police was reading the sports page of the LA Times, and just briefly gazed up. When Julian shot the door Lady G's eyes got big.

"You miss me baby?" Julian said as he laughed.

"You know I did!" Lady G said with a smile as she reach on side of the bed and grabbed the handcuff key and unhandcuffed herself.

Julian reached into his suit jacket and grabbed a nurse's outfit and a pair of white stockings and a pair of white tie-up Vans tennis shoes and gave it to Lady G to change into. Lady G took off the smock and slid on the stocking, nurses outfit and shoes while Julian stood with his back turned. She giggled at the thought and said, "I'm finished," and Julian turned back around.

"O'kay listen, I'm gonna call the police in here and after I draw down on him, you taser him."

"My pleasure," Lady G said as Julian handed her the taser and she covered it up with the patient smock that she took off.

"Excuse me office, can you assist me with this patient for a minute?"

"Sure Doctor!"

"Thank you," and the police officer put the news paper down and walked in the hospital room. As he walked in the room he saw Lady G sitting in the chair on side of her bed unhandcuffed.

"What the... how she get loose?" the police said as he looked back at Julian and Julian had a 3.80 automatic pointed at his head. "Hey buddy, what's going on?" The police asked as Lady G tasered him in the butt, and he fell to the ground shaking as Julian grabbed his gun and handcuffed him with his hands behind his back, and drug the police in the small restroom and he and Lady G made there way out the room into the elevator and out to Julian's rent-a-car.

Julian looked over after they got in the car and said, "I told you that I was coming to get you," and they hugged.

"What about G-Fly?"

"We got him too, now we can properly deal with our problems. But don't forget, we're fugitives now!" Julian said as he laughed and turned onto the main street headed toward the new safe house in Anaheim Hills. It was a nice 6 bedroom baby mansion that Julian leased through his attorney friend under one of his dummy corporations. Julian filled Lady G in on everything as they drove and when they pulled up to the new baby mansion, the girls already had G-fly placed in his new room that was converted into a hospital room. It had all of the high tech and fancy equipment that was needed to monitor G-Fly's condition. Big Bro and Dee Dee went to get rid of the stolen ambulance, and Julian introduced Lady G to the new retired register nurse that he hired to take care of her and G-Fly. The register nurse Joann was an older lady around 55 years old and worked as a nurse for over 30 years, so she knew her stuff. She was a little lady around 5' 1" and 105 pounds with salt and pepper hair and dark complexion. She retired because her husband died in a car accident in which she was the driver, and she lost her leg and now has to wear a prosthetic leg. Julian offered her $30 thousand dollars a month, and the deal was made. Joann and Cindy was good friends, so once Cindy told her about the situation then Joann was more then happy to help. She hated the police, because when she was younger the police shot and killed her big brother in cold blood. So to help G-Fly was more of a calling for her. Also, she introduced Julian to a retired Doctor name Doctor Brown who was 64 years old and well respected in his field. Julian gave the Doctor $200 thousand dollars plus put him on a $30 thousand dollar a month salary. And the doctor was sold on the deal.

Julian, Lady G, Princess, Tish, Gwen, Little Momma and Cindy was all in G-Fly's new bedroom listening to Joann explain how all of the expensive hospital equipment work, and the purpose of it. Princess and Tish was standing on each side of Lady G with their arms around her like they all was sister. Big Bro and Dee Dee walked in and they both hugged Lady G and kissed her on the cheek. It was obvious that they were all one big happy family and totally loyal to one another.

"Do everybody understand?" Joann asked.

"Yes, we got it!" Princess said as everybody else shook their heads in agreement.

"O'kay ya'll, Doctor Brown should be here shortly, so let's go have a moment in the family room. It's a couple of thoughts that we need to discuss." Julian said as they all went into the family room to have a meeting. As they all sat down Julian stayed standing as he begin to speak. "First things first, our brother Ty and little G will be properly layed to rest tomorrow. But unfortunately, we cannot attend the ceremony because we are now considered fugitives." And everyone looked disappointed and mad sounds to express their disapprovals.

"Julian that's my baby!" Lady G firmly stated.

"Yes, I'm aware of that, but you can bet that the police is going to be all around there, and you will be placed in custody as soon as they catch you. Now Ron is working on getting the detainers dropped, but until then, we got work to do and I'm sure that you want to participate! Right?

"Yes!"

"Well then, we got to put our love ones souls in Gods hands. Cindy will go with Ty's mother and father, and when this is over we'll all go and hold a special ceremony at their grave site. I've purchased a beautiful site on the hill and next to it, is ten more sites for our immediate family members, so we all can be together in the after life. So don't trip! I know that it's hard to not be there to say good bye, but we're going to be sure that our love ones rest in peace. O'kay, now that we got that understood, how do you feel?"

"Well I'm still a little sore! I had a c-section so I still got the stitches in me, but the doctor said that my other tests came back fine."

"Good! I know that this is kind of hard on you, but we've uncovered some vital information that I think you should become aware of. The incident was taped! G-Fly set up a secret surveillance system through the mansion that caught everything on tape, and we got evidence that the police planted a gun in G-Fly's hand after they gunned him down.

"Where is it at? I want to see it!" Lady G stated firmly."

"Are you sure you want to see it, it's very emotional..!"

"Don't baby me Julian! They took my life from me, and I want to see how and why they did it." Lady G said with a hostile tone in her voice.

"O'kay," Julian said as he walked over and put the tape in the VCR and pushed play.

"I don't want to see it again, so ya'll excuse me." Princess said as she stood up and walked out the room.

Gwen also excused herself and followed Princess out. Everybody else looked around to see if anyone else was going to leave, then looked on as the type started displaying the incident again.

When the tape was over everybody stared at Lady G as she set in a trans staring into the memories of her mind. "Lady G, Lady G!" Julian called her and interrupted her from her trans. Lady G looked up at him with tears running from her eyes. "Listen, we gave a copy to Ron and told him not to expose it to the media until we give him our approval. So he got it put up in a safe place until we finish our guest. If we reveal it now, then they will get arrested and we won't be able to get our revenge. You feel me?" Lady G shook her head. "Now we got a trace on officer Gust here." Julian then pointed at officer Gust on the TV screen. Lady G's eyes got big. I'm sure that he will be able to provide us with the information needed on his other friends.

"Where is he at?" Lady G asked.

"He lives in Inglewood and him and his friends here just got suspended pending investigation into this incident. So we got to be quick and discreet, because he might have people watching him too. Considering your recent escape from the hospital, you would most-likely be a number one suspect if any thing was to happen to him, so we got to do this right, you feel me?"

"What ever you say Boss!" Lady G said as she turned her eyes back at the TV screen and stared at her prey.

* * * *

Joe was sitting in his big Lazy Boy chair watching his two son play with their new Nintendo play station. he reached over and picked up the phone and called Gust. Gust little son Mikey answered it, "Hello!"

"Hi Mikey, this is our uncle Joe, let me speak to our daddy."

"Daddy telephone, it's uncle Joe…bye uncle Joe!"

"Bye Mikey!" Joe said as he smiled.

"Hello!"

"Hey Gust, what are you into?"

"Oh nothing, just enjoying a little family time with the old lady and the kids."

"Well I guess that it's about time, huh."

"Tell me what did Sandy say about the incident?" Joe asked.

"Nothing much, she's just glad that I'm safe. That's all..!"

"Well that's a good woman for you!"

"Yeah, I guess so! What did Debbie say to you? She don't ask no questions either, but I kind of told her bits and pieces just in case it turns bad, if you know what I mean?"

"Yeah I feel you."

"Anyway, I got that other hook-up and we need to go check it out tomorrow and see if we can take care of it."

"O'kay, what time do you want me to come by?" Gust asked.

"Say around 10:00 o'clock in the morning."

"O'kay, I'll be there."

"Cool, see you then!" Joe said.

"O'kay out! (click)

Joe hung up and called Fred.

"Hello," Fred answer the phone breathing hard with heavy medal music playing loud in the back ground.

"What's up stud! you must be working out." Fred recognized Joe's voice and said, "Hey partner, how did you guess."

"I know you, that's all!" Joe and Fred laughed.

"Anyway, I got that info, so be here tomorrow at 10 o'clock in the morning, so we can make it happen."

"I'm there!"

"Cool, I'll see you then."

"Alright." (click)

They hung up and Joe grabbed his can of Colt 45 and took a big sip, and watch his son's argue over who's cheating the most in the Nintendo football game.

* * * *

Officer Reeve, Officer Grant, and Officer Stevenson, all was standing in the Captain's office getting chewed out for allowing two very important suspects to be abducted from the hospital.

"Now let me get this straight," the Captain begin as he leaned back in is big leather chair. "A nurse approached you and asked you to assist her in dealing with a hostile male that was in the women's restroom. And when you arrived in the bathroom you seen two more women dressed as paramedics and the male suspect was sitting down on the toilet using it. And when you asked him to get up off the toilet and come with you, someone taser you both from behind and you woke up in the supply closet handcuffed and duck taped."

"That's accurate Sir."

And you were approached by a Doctor and asked if you can assist him with the suspect, and once you walked in the room the suspect was unhandcuffed, dressed, and sitting in the chair. And when you asked the doctor how she got unhandcuffed, he pulled an automatic gun on you, and then you were also tasered from behind and woke-up hand-cuffed and gagged in the restroom."

"That's right Sir!"

"Well gentlemen, since you guys can't handle the easy jobs, then maybe you need something much harder. I want all three of you to report to traffic duty immediately, and I advise you guys to get use to it, because you will be there for a very long time. Now get the hell out of my office." And the three officers walked out with their heads down.

"Detective Harris!"

"Yes Sir.," the detective stood up in front of the Captain's big oak desk.

"I want you to go visit lieutenant Adams and see how much information you can find out on these suspects, and I want everything that you can dig-up on them on my desk within 24 hours. They're getting a lot of help from somebody, and I don't like the fact that a common victim and patient who just lost her babies in a shoot out, just walk out of a hospital that's heavily secured. I want assault, robbery, and kidnap charges brought up on these suspects, and I want them hospital tapes on my desk too. Their Attorney just placed a multimillion dollar wrongful death law suit on this department and the State of California, and we cannot justify the raid or the shootings."

"Sir., the funerals tomorrow."

"I know when the officer's funeral is!"

"What does that have to do with the price of tea in China?"

"Not the officers funeral, but the suspect's funeral…the lady's babies."

"Oh yeah, I forgot about that, I want plain clothes police there with orders to arrest on sight. I doubt if she'd miss her own babies' funeral!   You go and oversee the stake out, we don't need anymore mistakes or problems. And watch out for the Media, they will be all over this."

"O'kay Sir., I'm on it! Detective Harris said as he hurried up and walked out. The Captain reached in his draw and grabbed a bottle of aspirin and took two, then leaned back in his chair as he ponder the situation.

Chapter 5
We Play 4 Keeps

The next day Julian, lady G and the crew was filled with sadness as they mourned the loss of their love ones and the funeral took place without them being able to be present. Lady G was trying to hide her pain as she walked around the mansion in a daze, humming the songs that she use to always sing to little G. Everyone felt her hidden pains, but didn't notice the inner rage that was strongly building in her soul. Her mind and heart was captured by her soul, and her soul was possessed by a deadly rage.

"Are you alright Babygirl?" Julian asked Lady G as he walked up to her.

"I'll be fine, just trying to gather my thoughts together."

"Well, if you want to talk, then we're here for you! Know that we all are family, and no one will be able to rest until we get revenge, and I promise you that we will get revenge for this or die trying!" Julian sincerely stated.

"I know J., and I believe you and love you for that! You've always been a strong leader and you've never ran from death, so I know that your thoughts are real. But I don't think that we will make it out of this one alive."

"Well if not, then at least we'll all be together and ride in the after life together." Julian joked as they both laughed and Julian held out his arms as Lady G melted into his strong embrace. Then he kissed her on the forehead and said, "We got business to attend to, let's go lay on our vic and see what we can find out." Lady G smiled excitingly as she rushed off to get ready.

* * * *

Cindy was at the funeral with Ty's mother and father, Ruby and Eddie, and although it was a fairly small gathering it was obvious that a lot of plain clothes police was lounging about trying to gain access and at the same time act inconspicuous. But Big Max was on point and his security team was keeping everyone who wasn't invited at bay. Big Max ran the youngsters security company that watched over the escort service and club, and his loyalty to the youngsters was unquestionable. Ty was always his favorite because of his rowdy quick to fight attitude, and to see Ty laying in a coffin broke Big Max heard and knowing the way Ty died, make Big Max furious. Big Max hated cops because he was a child who grow-up in the ghetto, but now, his hatred was a hundred times greater. Big Max stood at the entrance to the church with his clip board making sure no police made it into the ceremony. He also had workers at the back door, parking lot filming the ceremony, and filming all of the undercover cops that was trying to act inconspicuous. Ty's casket was sitting next to two baby caskets, one that held little G and the other that held Lady G's unborn child. It was a very sad sight to see and everyone in attendance was teary eyed.

After the funeral ceremony the caravan of limousines was escorted by an all white pale albino horse that pulled a carriage with Ty's casket on it, and on the side of the casket layed a black silk clothe that had R.6:8 engraved on it in gold writing. This was a secret code that the youngster's wanted displayed if one of them should die in battle, and it stood for Revelation Chapter 6: verse 8.

The police was looking all over the burial ground for any signs of Lady G, and was disappointed when they didn't find any. Detective Harris put a surveillance on Cindy, but this was anticipated, so Cindy already had an airplane ticket to Texas to go stay with her sister for a week, and then drive back when Julian call for her to come back. So after the burial ceremony, Cindy was driven to the airport in the limousine and jumped on her flight an hour after.

"Hello… Lieutenant Harris, yes, this is Detective Brown. She just jumped on a plane. Yes, to Texas! Do you want me to follow her? O'kay, I'll be back shortly." The police who was trailing Cindy hung up the phone, then watched as the airplane that Cindy just got on closed the door and started preparing for take off.

* * * *

Detective Joe, Fred, and Gust was on the back street to where the Asia dope dealers house was located. Joe looked over at Fred and Gust after putting on his bullet proof vest and blue DEA jacket and said, "Are ya'll ready?"

"As ready as we'll ever be!" Gust stated as Fred shook his head in a yes motion.

"O'kay then, we don't have no room for any mistakes, so watch your ass in there and shoot anyone who posing a threat. I want to be in and out of here as fast as possible, so let's get in and out." Joe put his black ski mask on his head, then they all exited the Bronco and walked through the yard that's opposite to the Asian dope dealers back yard, as they crept to the back fence and pulled down their ski mask.

It was 5:30p.m. and the sun was slowly setting. Joe, Fred and Gust jumped over the back wall and crept up to the back of the three bedroom house. Joe looked into the kitchen window and seen two Asian guys and one Asian girl counting money at the dinning room table, and another Asian girl was cooking something on the stove as they laughed and joked in their native tongue. Fred placed the crow bar in the crack of the back door where the lock was, and Joe held up his finger to give the three count, and when he got to two fingers, the Asian girl started hollering as she seen a glimpse of someone at the back door with a ski mask on. Joe said, "three, three, go, go!" And Fred busted the back door open as Joe lead the way and Gust ran in behind him.

One of the Asian guys grabbed his big 357 magnum off the table and started shooting as soon as the back door flew open. Joe ducked just in time as the first two bullets knocked big holes in the wall were his head was. Joe dove on the floor and was out of eye sight of his attacker, and when the Asian guy started toward the area where Joe dove at, Gust came through the door bussing his 45 automatic with the silencer attached and put four hot slugs in the Asian guy chest knocking him off his feet and back onto the table full of money. The other Asian guy came up with his Mac 10 spitting like crazy hitting Gust twice in the chest area as Gust fell into the back wall and jumped to the side where Joe pulled him quickly toward him, and Fred reached in side the door with his 9mm and started bussing wildly at the Asian guy. A bullet hit the Asian guy in the shoulder but he jumped behind a wall and reached back toward the back door and shot some more. Fred stepped back as the bullets riddle through the kitchen. The Asian guy Mac 10 ran out of bullets and clicked, and Joe and Fred ran toward him bussin. The Asian guy tried to run around toward the living room door, and was cut down as he was trying to open up the door. The Asian girls was screaming and crying as they seen their boy friends get shot down. "Shut up bitch, shut the fuck up before I shoot you!" Fred said as he drug the Asian girl who was under the table out next to the other one who was on the kitchen floor. "Lay there and you better not get up." Joe was getting the money off of the table as he pushed the dead Asian guy off the money and onto the floor. Fred started to help Joe grab the money, when they heard three loud pops and seen another Asian man fall to the floor around the corner from where Joe and Fred was at. Gust was standing in the cut with his gun smoking. "Go check the back room while I grab the rest of this." Joe said to Fred as he looked at Gust and said, "Watch his back, I got this!" Gust shook his head as Fred removed the Tec 9 from the dead Asian man's hand.

Fred and Gust crept through the house like combat soldiers, and then came walking back out with two duffle bags. "It's clear, and we found some more money and dope." Fred said.

"O'kay, let's get the fuck out of here before we have company."

"What about them?" Fred asked as the two Asian girls was hugged up crying quietly on the floor.

"Leave them, they ain't' seen nothing." Joe was referring to them wearing ski masks.

"O'kay let's roll!" Joe said as they ran out the back door and got to the back brick wall and Gust couldn't climb up because he got shot twice in his bullet proof vest in the chest area, and his whole chest was aching. So Fred and Joe push him up and over then threw the three duffle bags over and then jumped-up on top of the wall as they heard someone say, "Freeze!" They both looked as two police was on side of the house aiming their guns at them.

Joe and Fred didn't think twice as they both grabbed at their guns and started shooting at the two police officers. Bullets was flying over their heads and knocking holes in the big brick walls as they both jumped down and grabbed the one duffle bag that Gust left behind, as they ran toward the truck bussing back at the brick wall to keep the police from pursuing them urgently. Gust had the Bronco truck running when they jumped in and pulled away from the curve fast as the truck sped away and hit the corner before the police made it out to the street. Gust, Fred, and Joe took off their ski mask and Joe said, "There's no way that we can explain this, so if the police get behind us, then shoot to kill." And him and Fred started reloading their guns as Fred grabbed the two AK-47 from the back. Gust turned on the back street and Fred jumped out and put the license plates back on the truck, then jumped back in the truck as Gust sped back off then hit the corner as he turned onto the main street, then pulled onto the freeway on ramp. "How we look?" Joe asked.

"We're cool, I think we got away!" Gust said as they drove in silence.

Twenty minutes later, they pulled into the driveway of the motel that they rented earlier and parked, and laughed as they gave each-other high five and they got out of the truck and went inside of their motel room.

"Damn that was close." Fred yelled as he poured the blood stained money on the bed.

"You ain't lying. Gust, how bad is it?" Joe asked.

"I should make it, the bullet proof vest saved me." Gust said as he struggled out of his shirt, bullet proof vest, then T-shirt and seen the outline of two big bruises right next to one another on his chest.

"Boy, you're one lucky son-of-a-bitch!" Fred joked.

"We're all lucky today!" Gust firmly stated.

"You're not lying about that, it was almost over back there. I'm just glad that I had both of you guys watching my back, or I would've been fried rice back there!" Joe said as he poured out the other duffle bag of money.

"That's a lot of paper partner!" Fred said as they all gazed at all of the stacks of money on the bed.

"And we got four kilos of coke." And Gust pulled out a plastic pack of dope from the other duffle bag.

"That can't be a kilo, it's way too little!" Fred said from across the room.

"Let me see that! It is rather small for a kilo." And Joe took out his buck knife and stuck it into the dope, then tasted it and spit. "That's not fuckin coke… it's a pound of heroin! It's China white."

"Damn, that changes the game dramatically!" Gust said.

"I know, this stuff is worth a fortune on the street, at least a hundred thousand dollars a pound!" Joe said.

"No wonder why they got all of this money. Let's count it!" Fred said as they all started counting it.

An hour later Joe says, "That comes up to $668,000 thousand dollars."

"Damn, that's like $222,000 thousand dollars a piece." Gust stated.

"Yep, not including the money that we will make from this dope…we're rich!" Joe said and gave Fred and Gust both a hive five. "Listen, let's give Carl the 60 g's for setting up the lick, and that way he won't try to bet us out of the profit we'll make off this dope."

"I'm down with that."

"Me too!"

"O'kay let's split this money up so we can get the fuck out of here! " And Gust?

"What's up?" Gust looked up at Joe.

"Get rid of that damn truck!"

"It's on my priority list." Gust said as everybody laughed.

* * * *

Big Bro, Julian, Lady G, and Little Tish was all sitting inside Big Bro Astro Van down the street from officer Gust's house. "Are you sure that's his house?" Lady G asked Big Bro.

"Yeah, that's the right address." Big Bro said as he held up the piece of paper in his hand.

"Well, it's been over two hours and his ass ain't showed up." Lady G muttered in an pissed-off voice tone.

"That's why they call it surveillance… you suppose to sit back and patiently wait for your suspect to come." Big Bro said with a low chuckle.

"Why you say suspect? That sounds to much like some police shit. We need to change your vocabulary! Use Vic, as in victim." Little Tish joked.

"I know what Vic means!" Big Bro said as Julian and Little Tish laughed.

"Fuck vic, you need to say prey or mark!" Lady G said aggressively as everyone stopped laughing and looked at her seriously. "Listen, I'm tired of waiting! If that's his house, then I'm going inside to wait for him." Lady G said as she put on her coat.

"Wait Baby," Julian grabbed her by the arm. "What if it's not his shit?"

"Then we'll just leave after we make sure, it got to be some family pictures laying around some where to let us know." Lady G said.

"Big Bro, didn't you say that he just brought his daughter a brand new Nissan Sentra?" Little Tish asked.

"Yeah why?"

"Bingo!" And they all watched as a red Nissan Sentra pulled into the driveway, and a young blond hair girl got out with an older blond headed woman and a young boy, and they all went into the house.

"That must be his family." Big Bro said.

"Well let's go meet them then!" Lady G said as she got out of the car and started walking toward the house.

"Shit, come on let's go… Tish you and Lady G go in first and we're right in back of you."

"O'kay!" Little Tish said as she walked fast to catch-up with Lady G.

It was 7:15 at night, so it was vaguely dark but the street lights was on. Lady G and Little Tish walked up to

74

the door and rung the door bell. The older blond head lady looked out of the peep hole, and then opened up the door when she seen two black ladies, and as soon as she opened up the door and said, "Yes, may I help you?" Lady G socked her right in the nose knocking her to the ground, then her and Little Tish walked in and pulled their guns out as Lady G grabbed the white lady by her hair and drug her into the living-room. Tish walked in the back room and came back into the living-room with the young girl and little boy at gun point. Julian and Big Bro walked into the house with guns drawn. Lady G looked at Big Bro and said, "handcuff them to those chairs." And Big Bro went and grabbed three chairs from the dinning room table, then snatched the blond hair lady up and handcuffed her hands behind her back and through the nice brass chair.

"Get up and get your asses in them chairs," Little Tish ordered the girl and little boy and they complied.

"Why are you doing this to us… take what-ever you want, just don't hurt us," the lady begged.

"Shut the fuck up bitch! Where is your police husband at?" Lady G asked.

"I don't know! He doesn't live here anymore," the lady cried.

"Bitch, don't lie to me ... you don't want to see me get mad."

Julian was standing by the window and said, "We got company! That looks like him coming right there!"

"If you try to yell, then I'm gonna blow this little boy brains all over you, and that goes for you too!" Lady G said as she gazed at the young girl.

Gust got out of his truck and looked around for any suspicious cars or signs of police, and when he didn't see nothing, he walked toward his door. Gust opened up the door and walked in as he seen his family sitting in chairs and two ladies holding guns to his son and daughter's head. "Glad you can join us Gust." Julian said as he pointed a big 44 Bulldog at him.

"O'kay, don't hurt my family." Gust said right before Big Bro taser him. Gust fell to the ground shaking as his wife and daughter hollered.

Lady G slapped Gust wife and Little Tish grabbed Gust daughter hair as they both said, "shut-up bitch" and they both cried silently.

Big Bro took the duffle bag off of Gust shoulder and threw it to Julian, then stripped Gust of his two guns and handcuffed him behind his back and place some plastic straps on his ankles to tie his legs together. Julian opened up the duffle bag and poured out all of the money on the floor. "It looks like old Gust here has been a very busy person. Look its blood all over the bills. I guess Gust has been up to his old scandalous ways." Julian said as he looked at Lady G, then at Gust wife. Gust started coming to as Big Bro started slapping him in his face.

"Wake the fuck up, you muthafuckin scum bag!" Big Bro said as Gust looked up.

"Take the money, just don't hurt my family!" Gust said as he looked up at Julian.

"Well it's up to you if your family gets hurt or not. I'm gonna ask you some questions and I hope that you love your family enough to provide me with the answers that I need. Now, where do your partners Joe and Fred stay?" Julian firmly asked.

"I don't know, I just meet them at work." Gust said as Big Bro socked him in the face and busted his upper cheek.

"Wrong answer," Julian said.

"Quit playing games with him!" Lady G said as she walked over to the liquor bar and grabbed a fifth of Vodka and walked over and poured it all over Gust daughter.

The girl started crying loud as Gust wife started begging, "No please don't!"

"Now I'm gonna ask your punk ass again, where do your damn partners live at?" Lady G said as she lit a match.

"NO, No, please don't - tell them what they want to know Gust!" Gust wife screamed.

"I'm telling you, I don't know off hand but I can find out," Gust said.

"Wrong answer," Lady G said as she threw the match on the young girl and her clothes instantly went up in flames.

"Noooo!" Gust screamed as he watched his daughter jump around in the chair as the flames consumed her skin.

"Put it out!" Julian ordered as Big Bro ran into the bedroom and grabbed the quilt off the bed, and ran back and smothered the flames out, while Lady G laughed wickedly at the scene.

"You crazy bitch!" Gust wife yelled as Little Tish slapped her with the big 45 automatic and broke her nose.

"Shut the fuck up bitch, before I blow your fuckin head off." Tish uttered aggressively.

"Who are you guys?" Gust wife asked.

"Oh, you don't know? Your husband should know who we are. He came into my home and killed my babies and my brother, and put my husband on life support. I'm sure you heard about it! Now either he's gonna give me the information that I'm asking for, or I'm gonna burn this little bastard up next."

"Oh my God! Gust tell them what the want to know, please!" Gust wife pleaded.

Gust was in a daze because reality just set in, and he knew that his death was evident. Lady G waked over to the little boy with a bottle of whisky, and started pouring it on him as the boy started hollering and Gust said, "Wait, wait! Please wait! Go look on the bedroom dresser, it's a phone book on it with the information that you want."

Julian looked up at Big Bro and Big Bro went to retrieve the book. "Please don't hurt us any more, we had nothing to do with what happened to your family. I understand your pain, but this isn't the way to deal with it." Gust wife tried to reason.

"Oh it's not! Well what do you suggest? Lady G asked. The lady just looked down at her daughter burned up crying on the floor handcuffed to the chair, and just started to cry. Big Bro walked over and gave Julian the phone book and Julian flipped through it and shook his head.

"So tell me Gust, who sent you guys to kill us?"

"It wasn't supposed to go down like that. We just came for the money and dope."

"You didn't answer my question, maybe I should let her burn your little boy up so you'll know that I don't got time to play games," Julian said.

"O'kay please don't! It was a friend of Joe, he's from the Bay Area and he sets us up with licks on drug dealers and we split the money with him."

"What's his fuckin name?"

"It's Carl..!"

"Carl??? From Oakland!" Julian asked.

"Yes, he's a big drug dealer out of Oakland."

"Dark skin, tall, with gray hair?"

"Yes that's him!"

Julian looked over at Lady G an she shook her head as her facial expression couldn't hide her anger." Well Gust, I got some good news and some bad news for you. the bad news is, you and all of your crew will die because of the disrespect that you cause my family. But the good news is, Carl and his crew will join you guys shortly, and your family as well."

Gust looked up and said, "thank you as Julian stepped back and Lady G walked up. Lady G looked at Big Bro and pointed to his big Rambo knife that he wore on his side, and Big Bro pulled it out and handed it to her as she looked down at Gust then smiled, as their eyes meet and she said, "My brother taught me this! This is for my brother, husband, and babies," and she jumped on him and started stabbing him all up in his chest, neck, and head.

Gust wife, daughter, and son was crying hard as they witnessed the gruesome slaying of their father. "Lady, Lady! He's dead baby." Julian said as Lady G looked down and seen the bloody corpse laying motionless.

Lady G got up drenched in blood and walked over to Gust wife and said, "don't worry, your whole family is coming with you." Gust wife stared blankly at lady G as Lady G stabbed her straight in the heart and twisted the knife as Gust wife shook to her death. Lady G pulled out her 3.80 automatic and screwed the silencer on it then shot the daughter twice in the head then looked at the little boy as the little boy stared up at her and said, "I hate you!"

"I know!" Lady G said as she shot him twice in the heart, then empty the rest of her bullets in Gust lifeless corpse.

Tish had a wet towel in her hand as started wiping the blood from Lady G's face, arms, and hands.

Julian looked over at Big Bro and said, "grab the knife and lets go!"

Big Bro pulled the knife out of Gust wife heart and wrapped it up in a towel. "What about the money?" Big Bro asked.

"Leave it! Maybe it would throw them people off our tracks. Julian reasoned as they all walked out and closed the door in back of them. As they drove off Julian looked over at Lady G and asked, "Do you feel better baby?"

"A little..! But, I'll feel a lot better when we get Carl punk ass and the rest of them."

"Yeah, I feel you! We got work to do, so I want you to call a meeting tomorrow so we can put a plan together. It's time to turn it up a notch." Julian said as he blast a joint and passed it to Lady G with a smile, and said, "put it in the air!" And everybody laughed at Julian silly sense of humor.

Chapter 6
Scandalous Eyes of my Enemy!

Joe was up early watching the news when he heard his door bell ring. He looked over at the clock on the wall and it read 6:45a.m., it was too early for visitors so he knew that it had to be someone from the police force. He crept to his side window and didn't notice anybody lurking around and it was only one unmarked police car out front, so he walked to the front door with his big Dirty Harry 44 revolver in his hand, and peeped out of the peep hole just when detective Harris rung the door bell again. Joe seen that Detective Harris was alone as he opened-up the door. "What a pleasant surprise! What no cavalry?"

No Joe, I'm not here to arrest you, I'm just doing an investigation and I need some information from you."

"Is everything alright Joe? Joe looked back and seen Debbie standing in her silk robe in the living-room doorway clenching her automatic 3.80 Ruger."

"Everything's fine babe, it's just a friend from work coming to talk."

"O'kay, Debbie said as she went back in the bedroom. Joe and Debbie been married for 7 years, and Joe took pride in showing Debbie and his sons how to shoot guns and how to protect themselves. Debbie did home care nursing for old folks and protecting them from predators was essential to her.

"May I come in?" Detective Harris asked.

"Sure Mike come on in! Joe called the detective by his first name as he escorted him in and went to go sit at the dinning room table.

"Coffee?"

"Sure I'll have a cup... black will be fine! I apologize for coming by so early, but it seems like your suspects has escaped or has been kidnapped from the hospital underneath police protection, and the Captain is curious as to who these people really are. They have no police records, but have a lot of influence and high power attorneys on their side. So we need to know who we are dealing with and how you became aware of them?"

"Well Mike, as I've mentioned before, from what I understand, they suppose to be one of the biggest notorious drug family on the west coast. They allegedly supply 40 percent of the drugs that come into the California area. That's a lot considering that California's one of the biggest drug outlets of the United States, and I guess that my suspicion plays right, considering their power moves."

"How did you come about this information?"

Joe knew that he couldn't reveal this information so he tried to evade the question. "I got it from a confidential informer. Do you remember the Big Kingpin that just died name Game?"

"Of course, everyone has heard of him. 'The one that got away'!"

Yeah, that's what they call him! However, Mr. Tyquon the one that died, and Xavier, the one who was put in a comma are 'Game's young protégés. Ms. Davis is Game's old girlfriend who started messing around with Xavier when Game died, and that was their son that got killed and she was pregnant by him again."

"So Game's old girlfriend, started messing with Game's worker, who allegedly took over Game's empire when he died, and she had his son and was pregnant by him again." Detective Mike Harris surmised.

"Correct! Some sort of gangster incest or something. But they allegedly took over Game's connection and all of his clientele, so Game's empire never died, just his physical presence!"

"Well, why didn't you provide the department with this information, so we could've dealt with it tactfully, instead of you going out on a limb and trying to take them down all by yourself?"

"Well when Officer Steve gave me the information…!"

"Wait! Officer Steve Price provided you with this information?"

"Yes, it was his confidential informant and his investigation, and when we went to go check on it, then we notice suspicious movement and I decided to move in and play the hunch!"

"Well, it's real convenient that you went off of Officer Price investigating, when we just laid him to rest yesterday. So I guess that it's no way that we can verify these facts."

"Are you insinuating that I'm lying?" Joe said as he looked Detective Harris straight in the eyes.

"I'm not saying that you're lying, but I'm saying I'm sure a dead man can't say otherwise!" Detective Harris smiled then stood up. Don't worry Joe, I'll make sure that my report states these facts, maybe it can help you!" Detective Harris held out his hand and Joe shook it and they both smiled as Detective Harris said, "Thanks for the hospitality and I apologize for the early visit."

"No problem and Mike…! Thank you." Then Detective Harris smiled and walked out the door.

Joe shut the door and pace back and forth in his living room. "Is everything alright Baby?"

Joe turned and seen his wife standing in the doorway looking nerves. "Yes, everything is fine Kitty, just got to tie up some loose ends. Give me a hug!"

Debbie walked over and gave him a tight hug and said, "You promise that you'll never leave us Joe?"

"Don't worry Kitty, I'm not going no where. We got a long life ahead of us, so don't worry yourself, I got this o'kay!"

"O'kay honey! Are you still going to be able to take me and the boys to Magic Mountain today?"

"Of course Baby, ain't nothing changed. I just got to run over to Gust house for a minute. So be ready when I get back o'kay!"

"O'kay honey!" Debbie gave him a big kiss then went to wake the boys up.

* * * *

Joe pulled up at Gust house shortly after. He wanted to put Gust up on their new alibi about saying that it was Officer Price information that sparked the whole investigation. That way no body can find out who Price's informer was, and it would put a lot of weight on officer Price actions.

Joe knocked on the door and rung the door bell but no one answered. Both cars was parked in the driveway, so he knocked harder. But still no answer, so he went and looked through the little crack in the window and seen what looked like people sitting in chairs. "That's strange!" He mumbled to himself then tried the door knob and seen that it was open, so he pushed the door open then automatically grabbed his gun as he seen Gust's body disfigured on the floor, and Gust's whole family slaughtered. "What the fuck!" Joe uttered as he went through Gust's house with his gun drawn. He came back into the living-room and checked everybody pulse and knew by the way rigor mortise set in, that they had to be killed sometime yesterday night. Joe looked over and seen all the money that Gust made off the robbery laying on the rug next to the duffle bag. "They must've ambushed Gust when he came home last night. And if they didn't want the money then what did they want?" Joe thought to himself and then looked at Gust daughter and said, "Information! Gust and his family was tortured for information. This had to be Game's young crew, but who?" Joe knew that his time was limited because whoever tortured and killed Gust and his family wasn't playing, and obviously got the information that they came for. So Joe and his family might be next or Fred. Joe picked up the money and put it back in the bag, then put the duffle bag around his shoulder as he glanced at Gust and his family one more time, then walked out wiping his finger prints off the door knob. Joe jumped in his car then looked around as he drove off. His thoughts was racing as he called his wife and informed her to stay put, and do not answer the door under any circumstances. Then he called Fred but nobody answered, he hung up and called again but still no one answered. Joe hung up his cell phone then raced home.

* * * *

Julian was sitting at the head of the table with Lady G on one side of him and Princess on the other side of him, with Gwen, Dee Dee, Little Tish, Little Momma and Big Bro all in attendance. "I'm glad to see you all here today. As you know we are at war with a crew of crooked cops, and unfortunate for them we don't give a damn about no police, and we don't duck no rec! One of our brother is laying in the grave yard next to our god son, and our other brother is in there laying on a life support machine because of these crooked son-of-a-bitches. That could've been anyone of us in that cold grave yard, or laying there on that machine. And you know what? We will ride for you just the same, because we're your family." And everyone started clapping. "Now we ran across Gust punk ass and gave him and his family a nice going away party last night." And everyone started clapping and expressing their approval. Julian held up his hand to gain everyone attention. "And now we got a better understanding as to who our real enemies is, and why we are faced with this critical situation. So let me break this down for you. Game our mentor and god brother had a close associate from Oakland name Carl who's a big time player up there. When we first started working for Game, he took us up to Oakland to put in some work for his associate, because a rival dope dealer was threatening to take over his territory. So naturally, we went up there and laid some niggas down. But now this muthafucka Carl has establish himself a little crew and power, and feel that he can come and take over the territory that Game left behind. So he sent his police friend at us to take us out, so he can benefit off of our down fall. Now we know who the flunkies and the puppet master is, and it's time to show them who we are, and what we are about!" And everyone stood up clapping and shooting.

Julian waited until they quiet down and said, "Now listen! Princess, how much work do we have left?"

"We got 270 kilos left and I just took another three million dollars over to the other safe house."

"Good, just leave the rest of the dope at the safe house. We are effectually at war, and we need to concentrate all of our focus on these scandalous muthafuckas, because they are professionals and have resources that we don't have. So don't take them for granted, shoot to kill and stay with extra ammo. Now this is how we need to put it down.

Chapter 7
Death Has No Rules

Fred was on his way to the Family Fitness Center to get his ultimate work out on. He was on his new Ninja 900 motorcycle and feeling good after a long night of kinky sexy with two bad ass strippers. He had money to blow and he only had one objective, to live wild and enjoy life. He popped a wheelie as the light turn green and flew through the intersection. He looked back in his mirror to make sure no police wasn't on him, then he notice a black Vett and a convertible Porshe swooping through traffic trying to keep up. He smiled then slowed up a bit to see who it was and when he seen that it was ladies in both cars, he let them get closer so he can see how they looked. As the Vett and Porsche pulled up to about a car length behind Fred motorcycle two guns came out of both cars and Fred hit the gas on the motorcycle as the guns started bussin at him. The motorcycle sped away with rapid speed as one bullet gazed his helmet and another bullet shot his side mirror off.

"Catch that muthafucka," Dee Dee said to Princess, as Princess floored the gas peddle to the Vett and started trying to catch up with the motorcycle. Little Tish was right in back of the Vett in her convertible Porshe with Gwen, as Gwen was trying to get another good shot.

"Damn that motorcycle is fast."

Princess said as the motorcycle kept pulling away. Wait a minute we might have him he's slowing down for the next light.

Fred seen the light red in the front of him so he had to start slowing down as he down shifted, then skidded to a stop and pulled out his Glock 9mm and started shooting at his pursuers.

Princess and Little Tish seen Fred pull out his gun and start shooting so they both skidded to a stop 50 to 60 yard from where Fred stopped, and all four of them opened fired at him.

Fred stop in back of two cars that was waiting for the light when he started shooting, and when he seen the girls all start shooting back hitting the cars and window around him, he knew that he was out gunned and turned around and punched out through the red light. Tish and Dee Dee bullets caught Fred in the back of his shoulder and leg. And Princess bullet hit the back tire of the motorcycle, causing the motorcycle to flip over as it popped a wheelie through the intersection, and a big yellow school bus filled with kids hit Fred as the motorcycle flipped over causing the bus to drag Fred and the motorcycle for 40 yards before the bus stopped.

"Let's get out of here!" Princess said as she bust a u-turn and went the other direction with Tish trailing her. Both of their windshields had bullet holes in it, and Tish looked over at Gwen and Gwen was holding her shoulder while blood was running down her arm.

"You've been hit! Bitch why you didn't say nothing?" Tish screamed.

"It ain't nothing, it only grazed my shoulder," Gwen said.

"Let me see! That ain't no fuckin graze girl, we got to take you to the mansion to get you some help." Tish blinked her head lights on and off and Princess pulled to the side on a residential street.

"What's up?" Princess asked as Tish pulled on side of her.

"Gwen got shot in the shoulder, we need to take her to the mansion. Dee Dee call and see if Joann is there with G-Fly, and tell her that we're on our way. Princess I'll follow you!" Tish said as they pulled off.

They hit a couple of more side streets then jumped on the main street so they could jump on the freeway. As they were driving down Slauson Blvd. a police car seen the

Vett pass by him with bullet holes in the front windshield and busted a u-turn to get in hot pursuit of it.

Princess seen this and said, "Damn!" Then busted a u-turn and punched it down the opposite side of the street, and when she was passing by the police car she started unloading her 9mm into the side window of the police car causing it to swerve and wreck into the car on side of it. Princess and Dee Dee laughed as they sped off and turned the corner down Hoover then turned down a side street going back toward the freeway.

Tish seen Princess bust a u-turn and it caught her off guard so she kept straight, then she seen princess shot at the police car and the police car wrecked then tried to get in pursuit of the Vett, but Princess was gone. Tish and Gwen laughed as she turned onto the freeway headed for the mansion.

Tish got to the mansion and Joann was there looking over G-Fly, so she started taking care of Gwen's bullet wound as Little Tish was telling Julian, Big Bro, and Lady G what happened. The phone rung and Julian picked it up, "Hello! Damn Baby where are at? Good!" Julian looked at lady G and them and said, "It's Princess, they're at the safe house on 56th and Broadway," everybody smiled. "Yes, I heard about your work! You're going hard for the cause Huh? That's my girl. Ya'll kick back for an hour then take the undercover bucket and come here. I'll have someone go get your car and dispose of it. We love you too! See you later." Julian hung up the phone and said they'll be here later on. Lady G call Jake and tell him to go pick up the Vett in two days and dispose of it, and tell him to make sure he go at night.

"O'kay Boss!"

"And quit calling me that shit!"

"Whatever you say Boss." Lady G joked as her and Little Tish laughed and walked out.

* * * *

Joe told Debbie that he had to take her to her sister house until things blow over. She was arguing the fact until he broke down and told her about Gust and his family, and how he found them tortured and dead. She seen Joe cry for the first time, and knew that he was devastated. So she agreed to leave for a couple of weeks to appease him. Debbie packed her and the boys enough clothes to last them, and Joe gave her a suit case full of money that really scared her. She realize that Joe was in up over his head, and needed time to figure things out. He promised to come and get her in two weeks and they would start a new somewhere else, which made her feel better about the whole situation. Debbie sister stayed in Sacramento, so Joe went through the drive thru at Mc Donald's then stopped at an AM PM gas station to gas up.

"Listen Ms. P., I'm in position now and I'm about to make my move."

"Hold up B. B., we got stop by the light, we're not in position yet. Princess said through the walkie-talkie as she spoke to Big Bro.

"Don't trip, I got this P…!" Big Bro said into the walkie-talkie as he put it down and got out of the truck, and started walking around to the front of the AM PM gas station.

"Wait B. B., we're on our way don't leave without us, I repeat don't leave without us! Do you hear me? B. B. do you hear me?" Princess looked over at Little Tish and Dee Dee and said, "This nigga must've cut his walkie-talkie off."

"Green light, green light; GO..!" Little Tish said to Princess as she pulled her big 45 automatic out and took it off safety. Dee Dee cocked her box Uzi and Princess turned the corner driving in front of the AM PM gas station and seen Big Bro on the side at the pay phone with his hat down low and sun glasses on with a big coat looking out of place. Joe was in the AM PM paying for his gas and stuff. Debbie was in the car with the kids looking around at everyone who looked suspicious. Joe spooked her and she was paranoid a bit. Princess pulled in the laundry mat parking lot next to the AM PM gas station, and seen Joe come out and Big Bro turned and started coming toward him. Debbie seen Big Bro coming at Joe and yelled and blew the horn, as she pointed at Big Bro. Big Bro was startled by the horn and Debbie yelling as he looked at her and seen Joe's son's looking out of the window at him. Big Bro turned back toward Joe, and Joe was going for his big 357 magnum and Big Bro went for his Glock 9mm and they both started shooting at the same time. Big Bro got hit in the arm and Joe got hit in the shoulder and skinned on the side of his face as they both ducked for cover behind Joe's car. Joe was in front of his car and Big Bro was in the back of the car.

Princess and the girls seen everything going down in slow motion as they jumped out of the undercover bucket and started running over toward the gas station Big Bro had a clear shot at Joe through the back windshield, but Joe two sons was looking at him through the window so he didn't try to take it. Debbie yelled for her sons to lay down, and when they did, she came up with her automatic Ruger and started unloading it into Big Bro chest making his body dance as the bullets ate away at his soul.

"Nooo!" Little Tish screamed as her, Princess and Dee Dee unloaded into the side of Joe's car windows slicing away at Debbie's body and hitting Joe in the stomach and arm as Joe ducked on the other side of his car trading shots. Dee Dee ran up on the car and unloaded her clip into the interior of the car killing everything in it. Then reloaded as Little Tish and Princess was trying to finish Joe off. Joe ran out of ammunition and dove over to a car that was next to him, and a police car pulled up and skidded to a stop on the street by the curve and Little Tish, De Dee, and Princess turned their attention on the police car and lit it up, as the bullets riddle hard on the side of it. "Let's go! Come on let's go!" Princess said as they all turned and ran toward their car. Tish looked back and seen Big Bro laid out on the ground in back of Joe's car as she turned and ran. They jumped in the car and drove off as they heard police sirens in the distance. "Did we get him?" Prince asked.

"I'm not sure either, but I got his bitch." Dee Dee said as she reloaded her Uzi.

"How we look Princess?" Tish asked.

"I think we got away. Damn they got Big Bro!" Princess cursed. Then turned into an alley and parked as they pour gas over the bucket and lit it on fire, as they ran around to their other car and took off their wigs and sun glasses and drove off as they heard sirens in the distance.

When the second police car pulled up Joe was holding Debbie in his arms as he gazed in the back seat at his two slain sons. "Get on the fuckin ground! Get your ass on the ground Sir!" The police yelled.

"I'm a fuckin police got-damnit!"

"Show me your fuckin badge then!"

"I'm grabbing my wallet, don't fuckin shoot." Joe grabbed his wallet opened it up and handed it to the Rookie.

The Rookie looked at the ID and got on his radio and said, "I got a officer down at the AM PM on Crenshaw Blvd. I need immediate medical attention and back up. What happen Sir?"

"I was ambushed! That's one of the perpetrators laying back there. This is my family!"

The young Officer seen Joe's wife dead in his arms and two sons twisted and dead in the back seat and said, "Damn I'm sorry Sir."

Two more police cars skidded to a stop in front of the gas station and a paramedic. The young Rookie cop ran over and quickly brief the four other officers as the paramedics attended to Joes bullet wounds. Two of the officers knew Joe, so they ran over to help as Detective Harris pulled up and ran over to Joe while the paramedics was putting him on the stretcher and rolling him toward the paramedic ambulance.

"What happened Joe?" Detective Harris asked?

"They killed my family Mike!"

"Who?" Detective Mike Harris asked.

And Joe just stared in a daze as the paramedic's put him in the ambulance, and a tear ran down his face. "We got to go Sir., he lost to much blood and sustained multiple gun shot wounds." The young paramedic said as he slammed the back door to the ambulance.

"O'kay, I'll talk to him at the hospital..!" Detective Harris yelled as the ambulance pulled off. Detective Harris walked up to Joe's car and looked in and shook his head at the horrible bloody scene. "Don't touch nothing, tape this area off for the Forensic Team." Detective Harris walked over to Big Bro and lifted up his shirt and seen something that he didn't expect. It was a tattoo of a rare Special Forces symbol. "I'll be damn!" Detective Harris whispered. Because he knew that this changed the whole game. "Officer bring me a camera!" The officer ran to grab the camera as Detective Harris put on his gloves and searched Big Bro but found nothing. The officer gave Detective Harris the camera as he took four photos of Big Bro two Special Force tattoos. Then went into the AM PM gas station and showed his badge. "I'm seizing the tape to your surveillance camera."

"It's back here Sir!" The old Arab man said as he escorted Detective Harris to the back of the store.

"Rewind it and play it back for me!" Detective Harris asked the man as he complied and Detective Harris watched as the whole shoot out was played out on the monitor screen in front of him. {Damn, that was a professional hit, but who is these women?} Detective Harris thought to himself. "O'kay, I'll give you a confiscation form, and an officer will be here to interview you shorty...thank you for your assistance." Detective Harris said as he walked back out into the gas station. "Keep those News People out of here." The Forensic Team was on the scene now, and Detective Harris walked over to his old friend Detective Moto head of the Forensic Team and said, "Mr. Moto, this is a Class A Red file case, and I need as much information as you can on this case."

"No problem, we're on it!" Detective Harris glanced around once again then jumped in his car headed for the hospital.

* * * *

Princess, Dee Dee, and Little Tish ditch the bucket and went to the stash spot and changed their clothes and headed over to the mansion to tell Julian and Lady G the bad news. As they arrived at the mansion they went into the family room where Julian, Gwen and Lady G was sitting watching the news of the incident and Julian looked up and said, "What happened?"

"It wasn't our fault! He jumped the gun Daddy! We told him to wait until we caught up with him, but he didn't listen. The police saw him coming and pulled out at the same time and they both started shooting at each other, then they both jumped behind the police man car, that 's when we started running over there, but the police wife shot Big Bro through the back window of the car, and caught him slippin right before we got there. So we just opened fired on everyone! The police was ducking on the side of the car and shooting back, so we couldn't get a good shot a him. I know that we hit him, but I don't know if we killed him." Princess stated.

"I killed his bitch, I know that for sure. I got her ass! Dee Dee firmly stated.

"Listen Lady G!" And Lady G looked over at Julian. Get in touch with Little Momma and tell her to go and clean out and shut down the limousine and investigation service. Tell her to wear a disguise and I'll meet her there."

"O'kay, what are you going to do?"

"I'm gonna burn the office building down. We don't need any loose ends. And ya'll stay put, I'm sure that the damn gas station had surveillance cameras so I hope your disguised hold up."

"You know that we had on a good disguise." Little Tish said.

"I hope so!" Julian said as he looked at the scene on the TV showing the yellow tape and white blood stained sheet covering Big Bro body, and shook his head then walked out.

* * * *

Detective Harris was standing on side of Lieutenant Joe Adams bed side after Joe awoke from his surgery. Joe suffered multiple gun shot wounds one to the shoulder, one to the stomach, one to the arm, and one grazed his jaw leaving a noticeable scar. Joe I know that this got to be a hard time for you, but we need some answers."

Joe looked over and said, "I don't have no answers."

"Joe you don't have to fight this battle alone, we can help you!" Joe turned his head away from Detective Harris and stared at the IV that was hooked up to his arm. "Joe I know that whatever is going on is bigger then you, you need some help and you need to let us help you. "

"What makes you think that I need help now… it's too late for help! My whole damn family was killed before my eyes. How can you help that?"

"Just tell us who's responsible and we'll let the court system deal with them, and I'll make sure that they face the death penalty."

"Mike, they killed my whole family in cold blood. I am the death penalty that they face!"

"Joe you can't take them alone! If my hunch is right, they are more powerful then you think. The man that was killed at the gas station was a Special Force Navy Seal Expert." Joe looked over toward Detective Harris. "Yes, and I believe that it's more trained killers involve, because earlier today we found Gush and his whole family mangled, tortured and killed." Joe tried to look surprised, and if that's not enough to raffle your thoughts, then we just got through pulling your partner Fred's body from up under a bus. His head was severed from his body, and his body had multiple gun shot wounds in it." Joe eyes gave him away because he was really surprised to hear that.

Joe tried to regroup and said, "What makes you think that this incident was related?"

"Don't bullshit me Joe, and don't insult my intelligence! Whatever you guys did someone is very mad about it and they're coming for you, and they mean business. So do yourself a favor, and let us help you, and I promise you they will pay dearly for what they did."

"I don't know who it was!" Joe uttered.

"O'kay Joe, if that's the way you want it. But know you are not functioning as a officer of the Los Angeles Police Department. You are suspended, so your status and privileges is also suspended, so if you got caught breaking the law, then you will be held accountable for your actions."

"Are you finished?" Joe asked in an angry tone!

"Yeah I'm finished for now, but I have a feeling that we will be talking again soon. My condolences and I hope you over come your demons. There will be an officer posted outside your door until you're ready to leave, take care!"

Detective Harris turned and walked out the door as Joe was left staring at the ceiling over head. Detective Harris looked at the young police officer sitting outside the door and said, "Make sure that only the doctor and nurses that work on this floor, goes in this room, and make sure you check ID badges!"

"Yes Sir!" The young officer said as Detective Harris walked away.

* * * *

Julian made it to the Limousine and Investigation office that Big Bro and Little Momma ran, and Little Momma was already there packing up all of the documents and computers. She was dressed as a gang banger with a black khaki suit on, black high top all stars tennis shoes, a red bandana' around her mouth and chin with a black LA base ball cap. Julian almost didn't recognize her, as he put his gun back in his waste band and set the gasoline can down.

"What's going on J." Little Momma asked.

"I'll tell you later! Grab everything important and detrimental, and take it to your car."

"This is everything here!"

"O'kay, let's take it out! After they put everything in the truck of Little Mamma's BMW, Julian went back in the office and poured gas all over the desk, walls, bathroom and furniture and looked at Little Momma and said, "Meet me at the Mansion."

"O'kay!" Little Momma hurried out to her car and drove off as Julian lit a clothe that was stuffed in a bottle with gas in it, and throw it into the office door as he watch the flame ignite, then he ran around the block to his car and drove off as he seen smoke coming from the office roof.

Julian and Little Momma pulled into the Mansion driveway together and little Momma looked at Julian and asked, "What's going on J…?"

"Come in the house and I'll put you up on everything."

They walked in the Mansion and was greeted by the girls. Julian took Little Momma into the family room and told her what went down and how Big Bro got killed. She was deeply hurt by the news. Her and Big Bro went back a long ways and endured the most vicious circumstances and wars, that a combat unit could indulge in, and they always watched each-other's back and was down for one another like brother and sister. She dropped a tear and said, "Is the police officer dead?"

"No he's not! The news said that he suffered multiple gun shot wounds but is in stable condition," Lady G said.

"Well we need to finish the job!" Little Momma said with a serious look on her face.

"That's what I'm talking about, lets go get his punk ass!" Little Tish said as everyone of the girls agreed.

"Wait a minute! There is way too many police around that hospital right now. He might even be in police protection by now." Julian argued.

"Who cares! Really that's the best time, because they know that no body will be that bold as to try something now, and I won't let my brother die in vain." Little Momma firmly stated.

"Listen, we already kidnap G-Fly from that same hospital, so you know that they're on point and they might got video pictures of all of our faces. So it would be a foolish move!"

"They don't have my picture because I didn't go on that mission, so we don't have to worry about that, and I'm professionally trained for this kind of stuff, so I can handle it!" Little Momma argued back and all the girls looked at

Julian for a response as he got up and walked out of the room.

Julian went to the room where G-Fly was hooked up to the life support machine and all of the IV's and tubes running throw his body. Julian set down and Joann got up and walked out to let Julian have some privacy. "What's up my nigga! Damn, I wish that you were here with me now. I got so many decisions to make, and I don't know what to do. Big Bro just got killed on me and these crazy bitches is action all gun ho and invincible. It's getting ugly, and I don't think that we're going to live through this one. That bitch ass nigga Carl from Oakland is the one who started all of this shit. You remember him? The one we went up to Oakland and put in work for when we first started working for Game. Yeah, that coward nigga! He got himself a crew now, and he think that he can come and take what's ours. He got us fucked up, and I'm going up there and show his punk ass how we get down. Yeah rider style G-Red my nigga! If we don't make it back, then Joann got orders to pull your plug, that way you can be with us in the after life. It's us against the world my nigga... GP 4 Life..!" Julian said as he kissed G-Fly on the forehead and squeezed his hand then walked out.

Chapter 8
"Ride or Die"

Detective Harris was pulling a late night as he was analyzing the footage to the surveillance tape that he got of the shoot out at the AM PM gas station. He rewound it back and forth several times trying to get a good glimpse of the female shooters who killed Detective Joe's family. "Cold hearted bitches." Detective Harris uttered softly to himself, as he seen one of the female suspect shoot all into Joe's car with a Mac 10 killing Joe's wife and kids with no remorse. He played it back and notice that the male suspect that died had a clear shot at Joe's wife, but didn't take it because the two boys was in the window looking straight at him. Then Joe's wife gunned him down through the back window. Then a image of the three female suspects came from out of no where, as they ran up shooting like maniacs. He watched them shoot and seen that they wasn't professionals but knew how to handle a high caliber gun and was fearless.

He picked up the file of Officer Fred's death, and the witness report stated that the suspects look like four females in a Vett and Porsche, and they all got out of their cars and shot back at the motorcycle rider as he was shooting at them. The report says that the girls returned shots like they had no fear of getting hit. Detective Harris sat back in his chair and pondered the possibility. Then sat up and reached for the file on the kidnapping in the hospital. A nurse, two paramedic and a man sitting on a toilet in the women restroom. "Got to be!" Detective Harris got on the phone and called the hospital.

"Security records office please! Yes, is this the security records office? O'kay, my name is Detective Harris from the LAPD and I would like to see a copy of the surveillance tapes on the night of the kidnaping. I just want to view them for now, if I need them, then I'll get a court order. O'kay I'll be there shortly. Yes tonight! O'kay bye." Detective Harris hung up and phone as Sam walked up.

"Hey Mike, here's the information we found on your stiff down in the morgue. He was a well decorated bastard and highly trained for combat, but got kick out on some type of dishonorable discharge. It's all there but after his Navy records we have nothing else on him."

"O'kay thanks Sam!"

"The pleasures mine!" Sam said as he walked off.

Detective Harris scanned through Big Bro's files and said, "Kevin Brady, who are you, and why are you running around killing police?" Detective Harris asked himself as he looked at Big Bro Army picture then closed his folder placed it on his desk and left out.

* * * *

Julian was parked out side of the hospital with Lady G in his black 88 5.0 GT Mustang G-ride, as Princess was with Gwen in her 77 Cutless G-Ride, and Dee Dee was with Little Tish in her 86 Iroc Camero G-ride. They all was parked down the street from one another with walkie-talkies and disguises on as they watched Little Momma enter the hospital doors with her nurse outfit on and blond wig. "Maybe we should've sent someone in to watch her back!" Lady G expressed.

"No, because that might blow her cover if she has to help someone else get-away. She's professionally trained for this kind of shit, so let's just keep our eyes open and hope for the best." Julian said as he put in his N.W.A. CD and put it on his favorite song as he started reciting the lyrics "Fuck the Police! Fuck the Police!"

Lady G smiled and started singing the lyrics with him.

Little Momma looked around the hospital as she entered and analyzed everything around her. She seen the entrance to the stairwell right next to the elevators. She knew that Detective Joe was being held on the 4th floor, so she decided to take the stairs up in hope that she don't get any unwanted attention. She had on some all white Reebok tennis shoes with her white stocking and nurse outfit, and strap to her thigh was her trusty ice pick. As she made it to the 3rd. floor she walked in and realized that she was in the maternity ward. She grabbed a clip board and medicine tray that was laying by the desk, and walked away undetected by the other nurses. She jumped on the elevator going up to the 4th floor and two couples and a nurse was on the elevator with her. The elevator beeped and she got off in back of a couple and the nurse. Two police was waiting by the elevator door checking ID's and Little Momma heart dropped as she knew that she had to play it right. "Nurse, we need to see your ID?" The big buff officer said as Little Mamma tried to walk by.

"Oh, I'm sorry officer! Let me see, I'm sure I brung it with me today. Wow, I must've left it at my station. Doctor called me and asked me to bring this medication up for his patient that is allergic to Percocet. I'll just be a minute Sir! In and out I promise."

"O'kay, but hurry up!"

"I will, thank you officer." Little Momma said as she quickly walked away. She walked around the corner and seen a young black police talking to a nurse at the desk, and another one sitting by a door reading a magazine and knew that it had to be the door that Detective Joe was in, so she walked over and grabbed his folder off the wall and walked in the door as the young white Police jumped up and called after her as he walked in behind her.

"Nurse, nurse! Excuse me nurse!" Little Momma walked into the hospital room and seen the bed empty as the young police walked in behind her and said, "Nurse, your not suppose to be in here without authorization. Can I see some identification Maam?"

Little Momma opened up the folder and seen Lieutenant Joe Adam on the top page and the young black police walked in, "What's the problem Ed?"

"Maam, I said that I need some identification now!" The white cop repeated.

The door opened up to the restroom and Joe looked up and made eye contact with Little Momma as Little Momma reached up underneath her skirt and pulled out her ice pick and hit the first young white police in the forehead and pulled out the ice pick while the young black police was in shock, and spun around and hit him twice in the chest by his heart and up underneath his chin as he fell back against the wall. Little Momma grabbed his 9mm from his holster and Joe slammed the restroom door. Little Momma grabbed the pillow off the bed and shot through the restroom door as the gun shots muffed through the pillow. A nurse walked in and screamed at the sight as Little Momma tried to kick in the restroom door, but it wouldn't open. A police ran in with his gun drawn and Little Momma shot him twice in the chest through the pillow as his gun went off before he fell to the ground. The nurse ran out as Little Mamma unloaded the rest of her clip through the rest room door making a loud pop sound, then ran over and grabbed the police that she just shot in the chest gun, and ran out as the nurse was pointing at her to the other police and he shot at Little Momma as Little Momma dove behind the desk and the police bullet hit an old woman in the shoulder dropping her to the floor. Everyone was running and screaming as Little Momma ducked behind the desk as she ran around to the other end and jumped up, and shot the police right between the eyes. Then grabbed a towel from the nurse's cart and pulled the fire alarm down, and ran for the stair case. Everyone was running, hiding, and ducking trying to get out of the way as Little Momma ducked into the stairwell. A second later the elevator door opened up and three police ran through it into the commotion. Little Momma was running down the stairwell as other nurses was running in front of her, and a trail of police was coming up the stairs. They passed her by as she ran down to the bottom exit and out to the corridor of the lobby, and two policemen was stopping everybody trying to detain them in the lobby and when they got to Little Momma, she kicked one of the policemen in the nuts, and slapped the other one across his face with the gun, knocking them both to the ground as she ran out of the front entrance of the hospital.

Julian and the girls was waiting patiently in the cars as they seen two police cars pull up and skid in front of the hospital and four policemen ran into the entrance of the hospital. "We got movement!" Julian looked over at Lady G then pushed the walkie-talkie button down and said, "Look alive people!"

"Gotcha Baby!" Princess replied.

Three minutes later people started running out of the hospital and two minutes after that, Little Momma ran out the door with her gun in hand. A police car hit the corner and seen Little Momma running down the street and skidded to a stop right in back of her, as she turned around and started unloading the 9mm at the police car they jumped out behind their car door and opened fired at Little Momma. Little Momma jumped behind a park car as Princess and Gwen jumped out of their G-ride and shot the police down from behind. Little Momma ran and jumped in the car with Little Tish as two policemen ran out of the hospital shooting at Princess and Gwen as Little Tish handed Little Momma the AR-15 and jumped out with two 45 automatics and started bussin at the two policemen while another police car arrived, and Detective Harris in his unmark police cruiser. They all jumped out shooting at Little Tish, Dee Dee, and Little Momma as Julian jumped out with his AK-47 and told Lady G to tell the girls to roll out.

"Let's go, let's go….. NOW!!!"

"O'kay, O'kay!"

"Copy!" Princes and Dee Dee said, as they backed out and burned robber down the street. Julian unloaded his AK-47 into Detective Harris vehicle and the other police car as they dove underneath their cars, trying to get away from the deadly AK-47 bullets. Julian jumped back into his car and burned rubber down the street as Lady G hung out of the window unloading her Beretta 9mm at the police car tires. Julian hit the corner and the Mustang 5.0 engine was wide open as he hit a couple of more corners and jumped on the freeway. He punched it and the Mustang hit 120 mph easy, as he flew in and out of traffic then got off at the next exit and hit side streets until he hit the alley where the other cars was waiting. Him and Lady G got out and grab their guns as Julian poured gasoline through-out the car while Lady G was on the walkie-talkie.

They're on their way! Dee Dee pulled into the alley as Little Tish and Little Momma jumped out.

"Where's Princess and Gwen?" Little Momma asked in a paranoid voice.

"They're on their way, go get in the other cars." Lady G ordered as Princess hit the corner and pulled up. Everybody started hugging as Julian said, "Go get in the damn cars," and they all ran and jumped into the get-away cars. Julian finished pouring gas inside the car then made a trail from one car to the next, then he lit the gas and ran around to the get away car, "drive...get us up-out of here before the ghetto bird get here!" Princess punched out as Dee Dee trailed behind her. They drove to one of their stash spots and laid low through-out the night.

Julian looked over at Little Momma and said, "Did you get him?"

"I don't think so!" Then Little Momma started telling them what happened in detail.

* * * *

Detective Harris walked into the hospital room and looked at the two dead Rookie officers and the other police who was getting attended to by the doctor, his bullet proof vest stop the bullets but the impact knock the wind out of him. Detective Harris walked over to Lieutenant Joe who only got skinned by a bullet and said, "either you tell me what the fuck is going on, or I'm going to have you detained."

"Mike I told you the family that we hit and killed them kids, is a family of big time drug dealers…I'm talking kinpins! And this is the raft of their vengeance. They don't care about laws nor polices, and they will stop at nothing until they get revenge. I don't even know how they look or how many it is, but I'll guarantee you that if it takes my last breath, I'ma kill'em all!"

Detective Harris seen tears well up in Joes eyes and said, "Can you move?"

"I'll make it!"

"O'kay, follow me! I want to show you something." Joe stood up and fought though the pain as he followed Detective Harris through the hospital. They got off the elevator on the 5th floor and headed toward the security office department. Detective Harris held up his badge and said, "Can I speak to the supervisor?"

"That will be me sir!"

"I called earlier and requested the video tapes from the kidnapping that occurred."

"Yes Sir., over here!" And the old bald headed white man lead them over to the TV video screen and pushed play. They looked at the video screen and watched as the kidnapping was playing out before their eyes.

"Is anyone of them the woman that tried to kill you tonight?"

"No, the woman tonight looked Mexican or something. But you could tell that she had professional experience," Joe stated.

"Wait stop it there! Back it up a bit. Yeah, right there! Her,...I seen her tonight outside during the shoot out and they looked at a disguised picture of Dee Dee that kind of hid her features a bit. "Pull up the tape from tonight's shoot out."

Then the old bald head man complied as they watch the video of Little Momma as she creped through the hospital dressed as a nurse, and made it through the two officers' who was doing security watch on the floor. She walked up to Joe's hospital room boldly and ignored the young police officer as he tried to stop her and followed her into the room. Then the young black policemen walked into the room, then a nurse as she came back out running and one of the police officer that was on security post at the elevator ran over to help her and ran into the room also, then Little Momma came out of the room and the other policemen that was by the elevator shot at her and shot the old lady as Little Momma dove behind the counter, and came back up on the other side shooting as she killed the other police officer. Then she pulled down the fire alarm and ran with the crowd into the stairwell. The bald head white security supervisor pushed some buttons on the computer and the video of the stairwell came up as they seen Little Momma running down the stairwell with a towel covering up her gun and she ran right past the police officer's who was running up the stairs. As she got to the bottom floor two police officers was trying to stop and detain everyone who was running out of the stairwell, so Little Momma kicked one in the nuts, then spun around and slapped the other one in the face with the gun knocking them both to the floor, as she ran out of the hospital front entrance. "She's good!" The security supervisor said as Lieutenant Joe and Mike looked at him mean, then back at the video as the video man pulled up the outside cameras, and they seen the shoot out that occurred in the front of the hospital as her crew was outside waiting.

"Damn, these son-of-a-bitches is really crazy!" Detective Harris said.

"I told you!" Joe uttered as they seen the shoot out take place and how their crew was shooting down the police officers like they didn't care about the law.

"This got to be considered some form of anarchy!" Detective Harris surmised.

"Yep!" Joe uttered in agreement.

"Listen!" Detective Harris turned to the security supervisor. "I want a copy of both of these incidents."

"Sir., we're going to need a court order for that!" The security supervisor stated.

"I want you to look at all of these dead police officers and tell me that again!"

The security supervisor looked on the TV video screens at all of the dead and wounded police officers, then looked at his assistant and said, "Make the copies! Sir., you can just send me the court order at your convenience."

"Will do!" The supervisor handed Detective Harris the tapes and Detective Harris and Joe walked out. As they were walking down the corridor to the elevators Detective Harris stopped and turned toward Joe and said, "Joe, I know that these are some trying times for you and I would like to help you, but I'm sure that you're not interested in protective custody, so I won't offend you by asking you. These people are very dangerous and they want you bad, so you know what you're up against. Since you're suspended, I cannot officially help you, but since you are an old friend, then I'll do you a favor and make you copies of these suspects for you in hope that it may help you. Also, we found a large amount of money in the trunk of your car that had blood stains on it. {Joe eyes got big} But I'm going to delay that investigation as long as I can, so work quick and know that time is of the essence. I don't know what you where into or what you are hiding, but I have a feeling that it will all come out soon. So you better be prepared. Here's a hundred dollars you better creep out the back so the News won't see you, and good luck! You can pick up the package at Scotts deli tomorrow at around three o'clock. Detective Harris shook Joe's hand, and then walked onto the elevator as Joe took the stairwell out and caught a taxi cab home.

Joe got out of the cab on the street in back of his house, and jumped the back fence into his back yard and crept into his garage where some of his guns were stashed. He grabbed his M-16 rifle and gabbed two clips, then put on his bullet proof vest and grabbed his twin 45 automatics with four extra clips, and crept in his house looking to kill anything moving. After he check his house he checked the yard and street with his night vision glasses, and after he was content he went back into his house and planned, mourn, plotted, and planned some more, as he fell asleep with a picture of his family in one hand, and a 45 automatic in the other, with an empty whisky bottle on the table along side of him.

Chapter 9
The Way We Roll

It was the next morning and Julian was at the round table with his crazy ass devoted female crew. He looked around the table and said, "Listen Ladies! It's getting real hot around here and it's time for us to take a vacation somewhere until things cool off."

"I'm not going no where without G-Fly!" Lady G said in an argumentive way.

"I understand your love, and we all have the same love, but when G-Fly do wake up out of his coma, then you can come and get him, but if you stay, then you may never get to see him awake again. Now, before we leave we have some unfinished business up north that we must attend to, because I'll be damn if we'll leave without saying good bye. I want Carl and his whole crew dead within 48 hours." {And the girls started clapping to show their approval.} Now, I need you ladies to change your appearances all the way. {And he set some hair clippers on the table} Looks is not important at this stage of the game, because we are at war, and the police could possible have pictures, so we got to switch up a-bit so we can survive though this ordeal. Now we have a long drive ahead of us, so get yourselves ready and I'll be back in a couple of hours, I got some business to attend to. And Julian got up and hugged and kissed all of the ladies before he left.

Julian called up Ty's cousin Killa and met him at Killa's stereo and rim shop. "Yo, what's up big homie!" Julian said as they both embraced.

"Same shit young gangsta, just a different day! It's good to see you J., you know that your still my little cousin…you can still come and see a nigga sometimes."

"Man it's been a lot of crazy shit going on!" Julian uttered.

"Yeah I know, I've been watching the News. Is that your work?" Killa inquired.

"Let take a ride and I'll share some game with you… I need your help anyway."

"Anything you need little bro., let's roll!" Killa said as they hopped in Julian's rent-a-car and rolled out.

Julian said, "check it out! The police that killed your cousin was as crooked as they come. A big time nigga from the Bay Area sent them at us so he could get us out of the way. After we got word of this, we went hard, and that's what you see is going down now!"

"Damn little nigga, ya'll warring with the popo?"

"You muthafuckin right, they killed my nigga in cold blood and put G-Fly in a coma on life support, and killed little G and the baby Lady G was carrying, so you got-damn-right it's war. Fuck them bitches, they can bleed and die like us. They ain't untouchable!"

"I feel you my nigga, and I respect the hell out of you for that. Ty was my little cousin, and he always made sure that I ate good when he came up, so you know that I got your back to the fullest. What you want to go kill one of them bitches now?"

"Naw, I got that! But what I need from you is, for you to move some weight for me because me and my crew got to lay low for a minute."

"That ain't no problem, I got a couple of people who will take 20 or 30 of them off your hands right now, if you want me to call them?"

"No, I'm going to just give you the work and pick up the money from you later. All I want is twelve thousand a bird."

"That's love!"

Julian pulled in front of is stash spot and told Killa to come on as they went in. Julian closed the door and said, "Come on." As he lead Killa in the back bedroom and opened up the closet and it was filled with keys.

"Damn, how much is that?" Killa asked.

"About 270 kilos, give or take a few! Can you handle it for me?" Julian asked.

"You muthafuckin right I can handle it! How soon do you need the money?"

"Take your time! I already got another stash spot for you over in Hollywood Hills that you can take the money. Here is the address and keys to the house, and these keys is for this house. It's a 79 Buick Regal in the garage that's clean, it's low key and runs good, so use it if you need it. The rent and bills is paid up and either me or Lady G will contract you. O'kay?"

"Cool, I got you! And peep, it just dawned on me that I met some niggas from the Bay Area down here selling weight. He gave me his number but I haven't called him yet. You want to snatch him?"

"Naw! I got bigger fish to fry, you take care of him, and consider it a going away present to Ty!"

"You got that..? That's my word!"

"Much respect homeboy! Let me drop you back off so you can paper chase." And they laughed as they walked out.

Joe woke up at noon with a massive hang-over his head was pounding as the sound of the phone ringing amplified the pounding. He looked around at everything as reality set in and he clinched his 45 automatic as he scanned his surroundings looking for intruders. Then he picked up the phone.

"Hello!" It was Melony his wife Debbie's younger sister.

"Yes, Melony it's true! I was going to call you today and tell you, but I was up all night and I just woke up." {Melony was crying hard on the other end and Joe's eyes started to water as the pain hit him again.}

Melony, Melony! I need you to pull yourself together. I need you to come and prepare the funeral arrangements for me. O'kay? I'll drop some money off to you today to cover it, and bring you the information you need to located Debbie and the kids. What am I going to do? I'm going to kill the ones who did this to my family."

Melony was telling Joe to let God deal with it, as Joe gently hung up the phone in her face. "I am God now!" Joe whispered as he got up and went to get dressed so he could go take care of his business.

Julian, Lady G and Little Tish was in Julian's big Chevy Blazer truck and Princess, Gwen, Dee Dee, and Little Momma was in Princess convertible Iroc as they both caravanned on their way to Oakland California. Oakland was a seven our drive from Los Angeles, and Julian was making sure that he went the speed limit because he couldn't chance getting pulled over because they all was probably fugitives by now, and if not then, all the guns in the vehicles would for sure be hard to explain. Julian looked over at Lady G who was in the passenger seat bouncing her head to the music, then he looked at Little Tish who was in the back seat looking out of the window doing the same. Julian laughed to himself as he pictured them all with their new bald head hair cuts. Princess, Dee Dee, and Lady G looked more butch trapped in a thick feminine body, and Little Tish, Little Momma, and Gwen looked like beautiful models with the exotic baby face and sexy woman body. But all was heartless killers. Julian smiled and said to himself, "What a cold combination!" Julian cut down the music and said, "Check it out ladies," and Lady G and Tish looked over at him and gave him their full attention. Julian was a young boss, and they all respected him as one, and will kill and die at a drop of a dime for him. "We're about to go into territory that we are not familiar with, so I think that we should take a day or two to scope out the area and Carl's operation. We'll have one of the girls go grab an apartment so we can lay low, and some cars from the auto trade paper. It's to late in the game to start moving sloppy. We don't have to snatch him and torture him, just kill him and move on." {And he looked over at Lady G, knowing that Lady G had intentions on torturing Carl for what he done to them.} "Do I make myself clear on that?"

"Whatever you say boss!" Lady G said in a sarcastic way.

Julian shook his head as Little Tish was trying to cover up her sound as she laughed.

* * * *

Joe walked into photography and tattoo shop on the Westside of Los Angeles and seen Troy Smith, and ex-con who specialize in credit cards and fake ID scams." Troy what's good player, long time no see!" Joe busted Troy before and Troy did an 18 month bid in Terminal Island Federal Correctional Institution because of it.

"Nothing much, just trying to make an honest dollar or two!" Troy said as he opened up his arms in reference to his legitimate shop.

"Yes this place is nice, and a good front if I may add!"

"I'm strictly legit now, and I pay my taxes, so if you ain't got a search warrant, then you can see your way out."

"Troy, Troy, that ain't the way to speak to an old friend, now is it? I came to do business with you!" And Joe reached in his pocket and pulled out a wod of bills and set it on the counter.

"What is this, some type of joke? What you trying to entrap me or something?" Troy said as he looked at the money.

"No, I'm straight on the up and up!"

"Well, I don't do that no more, and if I did, then I wouldn't do it for no fuckin police!" Troy said with malice in his voice.

"Oh yeah, well how about I take a little look around here… you know, to make sure that you're really on the straight and narrow!"

"I know my rights, you need a search warrant for that!"

Joe smiled as he pushed his way through the back room where the photo shoot was set up at. "I see that you have very expensive equipment back here, you got to take quality pictures with this. Oh what's this?" And Joe reached into his coat pocket and pulled out a baggy full of Heroin. "Look what I just found, two ounces of Heroin! That's like 20 years to life in prison for you Troy."

"Man, that ain't my shit, you just pulled that shit out of your pocket."

"Who do you think that the judge gonna believe, me or you?"

"Man this is bullshit!"

"Listen Troy, all I want is a fake ID and you can keep the money and I'll be out of your hair, but if not, then you'll spend the rest of your natural born black ass life in prison wishing you would've."

"O'kay, o'kay! Come on man bring your ass over here, and I don't want to ever see your crooked ass again. Stand over there against the wall." Joe complied as Troy took his photo and punched his keys on his computer as he said, "What name do you want?"

"James Hart!"

"That fuckin name fit you too!" Troy said as he pushed some more buttons and went over to the laser printer and retrieved the ID and handed it to Joe. "Here!"

"Nice work! Here's a tip." And Joe handed him the dope and walked out as Troy stared at Joe, then the dope in a confused way.

Joe went and rented out a one bedroom apartment in his new alias name, then swung by Scott's Deli on the Westside to pick-up the information that Detective Harris left him. Scott was and old retired police officer who got his leg shot off during a bank robbery back in the day, and he took his money and opened up a deli so he can cater to his fellow officers and provide a place where they could kick it at and watch the ball games on their day off. Scott served beer and wine, so his place was always pretty full.

"Look what the wind has blown in. It's good to see you Joe and my condolence to your family."

"Thank you Scott!"

"If there is anything that I could do for you, then don't hesitate to ask. Sally, make my friend here one of those roast beef specials to take with him."

"Will do!"

"Thank you Sally!"

"Anytime Joe." Sally said with a smile.

"Come on Joe, let's go to my office I got something for you." And Joe followed Scott as Scott limped to his office. Detective Harris left this for you. Also, if you need to contact him, then you can go through me, here's my pager number and the number to the deli. If I can help you with anything else, then just ask. Listen Joe, fighting crime is a dirty job, and sometimes we all got to get dirty in order to survive. So don't think you don't have no friends, the one's who talk bad and opposes the dirty cop, is really the dirtiest cop! So don't you forget that! You need guns or back up let me know. Our people stick together during the struggles. You hear me?"

"Yes Sir., and thank you!"

"No problem, now go handle your business!" Joe shook Scott's hand then turned and walked out.

* * * *

Julian, Lady G, Little Momma and Gwen was sitting down the street from Carl's pool hall watching the activities as people came and went. You could tell the pool hall catered to the young hustlers because of the cars and women that came and went. Dee Dee, Little Tish and Princess went to rent an apartment with their fake ID's and brought some low key buckets out of the Auto Trade, so they could have some vehicles to put down the hit in and not draw any suspicion on their other vehicles.

"Look J., ain't that him?" Lady G asked.

"Yep, that's that muthafucka! And those other two nigga must be his body guards." Julian said as he seen a big man and a little buff man getting out of the front seat of the new Cadillac Fleetwood Brougham, then the big man opened-up the back door to the Cadillac to let Carl out as they both walked on side of Carl as they entered the pool hall.

"I say that we wait until he come out and gun him down now and get it over with," Lady G expressed.

"No we stick to the script, see if we can trail him. He ain't no fool and he's a cold blooded coward, so that means he's extra cautious. And he knows that we might be coming, so he's probably kind of prepared. That's why he got two body guards now!"

"Julian, I don't give a damn about no body guards!" Lady G firmly stated.

"I feel you on that, but you need to start caring about your family, because they will follow you blindly to hell if you lead them that way. So honor your obligations to us, and play your muthafuckin position, and let me play my part!" Julian scolded as the whole track got quiet.

"Daddy do you want me and Gwen to go in and look around?" Little Momma asked.

"No, it might be too risky! He knows that Game owned an escort service, so he might become suspicious if he seen two bad ass bald headed bitches walk in there that's not from this area. {And he smiled at them as they blushed at the compliment.} Let's wait until he leaves so we won't arouse his fears.

"O'kay." Little Momma agreed.

Lady G looked at Julian and shook her head and laughed.

"What..?" Julian asked.

"Oh nothing, I was just thinking about how far you came in such a short time. I see that Game taught you well."

Julian smiled, then seen Carl walk back out with his two body guards and jump in his Cadillac.

"There he goes!" Julian said as he started the truck and started following the Cadillac. They drove down the ghetto streets of East Oakland and pulled up on a street where niggas was out and about hustling on both sides of the street. Julian turned off so he wouldn't be notice following the Cadillac, and went down five blocks then came back up the other way but the Cadillac was gone. "Damn! Where did this muthafucka go?"

"He's gone J., we'll catch up with him later. Let's go get something to eat, I'm starving!" Lady G said to ease the mood. Gwen caught on and said, "Me too!" Julian looked at Lady G and just shook his head as he drove off. Lady G just smiled to herself.

* * * *

Joe when to his old house and grabbed majority of his guns, money and some clothes and took them to his new apartment for safe keeping. Then he sat on the floor and ate his roast beef sandwich as he scanned through the pictures and information that Detective Harris sent to him. He looked through all of the pictures carefully, and seen that all of the females look identical to the females on each incident. "Damn, these are the same females on each offense. They just disguise themselves differently. Joe whispered to himself as he opened up another legal envelope that had an X on it. It was the information on Big Bro and pictures at the shoot-out of the AM PM gas station that his wife and kids got killed in. It was a picture of Debbie shooting Big Bro through the back window of the car. He gazed at his loving companion and his eyes got blood shot red with pain. He looked at the other picture and it was a photo of the three ladies running up on his car shooting at him and his family. His memory reflected back to the scene of the crime as his thought played back the incident in his head. He heard the gun shots from the Uzi echoing though his ears, as he heard Debbie scream a pain that was different then getting shot or dying. It was the scream of seeing your babies get slaughtered in cold blood. Joe snapped out of his trance and stared deeply at the armed females in the photo. He then picked up the military file that he had of Big Bro and started reading it. It said that Kevin Brady and his unit Sergeant Latoya Deazee got court martial and received a dishonorable discharge. Joe thought about it then said, "Got to be!" Then picked up his cell phone and called Scott's Deli. Scott pick up on the third ring and said, "Scott's Deli..! Scott speaking, how can I help you?"

"Hey Scott, this is Joe!"

"Joe, what's good?"

"I need a favor!"

"What can I help you with?"

"I need you to run a name for me! Her name is Latoya Deazee!"

"Got it."

"If nothing shows up in the NCIC then tell him to run a military check, she's a sergeant."

"Will do, call me back in a couple of hours."

"O'kay, thanks Scott!"

"No, problem, that's what friend are for. Holler at you later."

"O'kay." {click} Joe hung up the phone and stared at the photos on the floor.

* * * *

"What's up Cuz, yeah I need twenty! Is that to much for you? Well listen, where ever you trying to meet is cool with me. Yeah, you can count the paper first... I'm not trippin' that. But you better be on the up and up Cuz, I ain't got time to be playing. Cool, I'll be their in an hour. Later!"

He wants me to meet him at the Travel Lodge Motel on Western. He wants to count the money, so I'ma let him count the money to ease his suspicion. Then when he bring the work in I'll give him the money, and when we leave, I want ya'll to smoke them fools and get my money back. He's gonna have some of his homies in the cut so watch your back, and smoke them fools too. Ya'll down or what?"

"Hell yeah, we down!" Killa three little homeboys said with excitement in their voice.

"Good, ya'll put this down for me, then I'ma make sure you be ballin' before the week is up. But don't tell nobody about this! Take this shit to your muthafuckin grave nigga... you feel me Cuz?"

"We don't do no talking big homie!"

"Good!" Killa unzipped a big duffle bag and it was full of guns. "Grab what you need little nigga, because it's about to go down."

They all started grabbing the guns that they desired. All three of them was 15 years old and gang bangin' was all that they knew and lived for. Killa had been lacing them for a year, and they been buying ounces from him to hustle and keep money in their pocket. Killa told them that one day he was gonna put them on so they can make some real money, but they got to prove that they're down and loyal to the cause, and they were all anxious to prove their loyalty and heart. They reminded Killa of Ty, G-Fly, and Julian, but not as suave with their demeanor. They all was from 120th Ramond Crip, and Killa was the big homie and baller of the neighborhood, so they respected and admired him. The tallest name was Slim C, he was 6'3" skinny dark skin with long braids. The second one name was Big Boy, he was 5'8" 240 lbs., with a strong pudgy built. He was light skin with short natural wavy hair. The third one name was Little RC, he was 5'6" medium built, brown skin with a short fade and the wildest out of the three, Slim C grabbed the box Uzi and a 357 Magnum out the bag. Big Boy grabbed two chrome twin 45 automatics, and Little RC grabbed a Tec 9 and a 44 Bulldog Revolver. Killa had a glock 9mm and a big 357 Magnum with a six inch barrel. He looked at his little homies and said, "I want Slim and Little RC to drive the Mini Blazer, and Big Boy you drive the Trans Am and watch our backs. Ya'll stay outside, and if they come out with this Nike bag without me, then get to shooting, because they pulled a fast one and caught me slipping."

"Gotcha."

"Don't worry big homie we got your back." Little RC said as he clenched his new toy.

"O'kay then, let's roll..!"

Killa pulled up to the Travel Lodge Motel with Slim and Little RC trailing behind him. He seen Cash the dude that he met from Oakland standing in the doorway of the motel room and he had another light skin dude with him. As Killa got out he seen another dude sitting on a new Lincoln Mark Seven with his diamonds glistening in the Sun. Slim parked parallel to dude in the Lincoln Mark Seven and Killa smiled at this little homies being on point. Their motel room was toward the back of the parking lot so

Big Boy parked closer to the exit so he can see everything coming and going, and still have a birds-eye view of his homie at the back of the parking lot.

Killa walked up with the Nike duffle bag on his shoulder. "Come on in player, it's all good!" Cash said with a player grin. "I didn't think that you was gonna come."

"Well my connect got taken out of the game, so I'm looking for a new connect." Killa said as he looked around. "Is it just ya'll two in here?"

"Yeah, our other people is outside!" Cash said.

"Do you mind if I look for myself?"

"Naw, go right ahead. We're on the up and up." Cash said as Killa kept his hand clenched on the butt of his 357 Magnum as he looked in the bathroom and then the closet and seen that they both was empty. Cash and his partner both kept their hands on the butt of their guns as well. "Satisfied?"

"Yeah, here!" And Killa set the money on the table and set down to ease the tension. Cash partner stood against the back wall posted as Cash started going through the stacks of bills making sure that it was real money. "It's all put in five thousand dollar stacks, so that should be easier for you to count."

144

Cash shook his head, then picked up two stacks and counted them and when he seen that they both was accurate, he counted to see how many stacks it was. "How much is in here?" Cash asked.

"$270,000 dollars!"

Cash knew that that was right, so he looked at his partner and said, "Go grab the yayo." And his partner opened up the door and went to the car. "I better let my homies see me before they think the wrong thing and get to shooting." Killa stepped in the door way so Slim and Little RC could see him and walked back in as Cash partner brung the dope in. He set it on the table next to the money and Killa started checking each kilo then took one from the bottom of the bag and stuck his buck knife in it and tasted it.

"Don't worry player, we stand on our work!" Cash said with a smile.

"Good, and if my people like it, then I'll be hitting you up often."

"Cool player give me a call whenever you need me, I got you."

They shook hands and Killa walked out with the duffle bag full of dope on his shoulder and hand on the butt of his gun.

"He's out already let's get at these niggas." Little RC said as he clenched his new Tec 9.

"Wait a minute nigga, let the homie pull out first." Slim yelled.

Cashed and his partner walked out of the motel room in back of Killa and jumped in their BMW and as soon as they got in their car, another nigga walked out of another room next to the nigga in the Lincoln Mark Seven, and he was carrying a pillow case with an AK-47 in it. See nigga it's good to be patient some times. Killa pulled out and Slim said, "When I move on the Lincoln you move on the BMW."

"Gotcha Cuz."

Slim pulled out in back of Killa then slammed the Mini Blazer in park, as he jumped out with his 357 Magnum sparking. The first three shots hit the dude with the AK-47 in the back of the head blowing his brains all over the front windshield as the big caliber gun had no mercy. The second man tried to jump back up out of the car, but he was too late as the two 357 Magnum bullets tore at his back. Slim raised the Uzi and finished him off as he slid onto the ground shaking to his death. Little RC was shooting wildly with the Tec 9. He hit Cash multiple time and Cash partner jumped out of the car running low and shooting back at Little RC and Slim. He caught up to Killa's car and aimed his 9mm and didn't see Big Boy between the park cars, as he ran out and unloaded both 45 automatic into Cash partner's body. Slim ran over and grabbed the money out of the BMW and they hopped back into the Mini Blazer and punched out as they all caravanned back toward the hood. Killa lead them to an alley in Blood Hood, and they throw gasoline in the Mini Blazer and Trans Am and lit them on fire, and as they were pulling out of the alley, some Bloods came out bussin' at Killa's 76 Monte Carlo as he burned rubber up out of there. "Cuz we should've served them Blood niggas." Little RC shouted.

"Nigga we got too much at stake to be shooting it out with them clowns, I'm trying to get money, I'm tired of being broke and fucked up," Slim expressed.

"That's right my nigga give his young crazy ass a reality check! If it don't make dollars, it don't make sense. It's about getting this money now young nigga, so keep your guards up, but concentrate on stacking a grip. You feel me Cuz?"

"Yeah we feel you big homie." Big Boy said as they pulled up in one of Killa's low key spot.

They got out and grabbed the duffle bags and followed Killa in the house. Killa put the duffle bag with the money on the table and Big Boy set the duffle bag with the dope on the table too. Killa opened up the duffle bag with the dope in it and started pulling out bricks of cocaine. He separated three stacks of six kilos and through a stack of bills on the table and said, "That's six kilos a piece and 5 g's that ya'll can split, so you can have some money in your pockets to hold you over until you start getting rid of the dope. It's an 85' 300ZX Nissan out front that ya'll can have, and ya'll can take over this spot until you get yourself together. No one knows about this spot but you and me, so I hope that ya'll keep it like that. I'm going to get rid of these guns so we don't get caught up. Its two guns in the bedroom dresser that ya'll can have. It's time to get money, so be smart and stack your ends. The object is to get rich not act rich, and when ya'll are ready to re-cop, then give me a call. Any questions?"

"Naw big homie... thank you Cuz!" Big Boy uttered.

"Yeah, much respect triple OG!" Slim C said as everyone smiled.

Little RC said, "I'm speechless Cuz! Much love!"

"You know what they say, real niggas do real things, and fake niggas always get exposed. So play you part! I'm out!" Killa smiled and walked out with the money two kilos and a duffle bag full of hot guns.

Chapter 10
Gangsta 4 Life

Detective Harris ran Latoya Deazee through NCIC data base but nothing came up because she didn't have any criminal background. So Detective Harris ran her name and military title through the military data base background computer, and her profile came up with her military accomplishments and her dishonorable discharge reference. But it didn't show no indication why she receive a dishonorable discharge. Detective Harris punched in a request for her dishonorable discharge information and it came back classified information. Detective Harris stared at Latoya Deazee photo and said, "This got to be her!" As the resemblance to the female suspect that was involved in the hospital shooting was very similar. "Good work Joe!" Detective Harris whispered as he went to make copies.

Detective Cannon walked up as Detective Harris was making copies and said, "Mike I think that you might find this information relevant to your case. We recently had a arson at an office building in the Slauson Shopping Center at a Limousine and Investigation Shop, and we recover a latent fingerprint of your suspect that got killed in the AM PM gas station shoot out." {Detective Harris eyes got big.} And not only that, we found a burned up receipt for the installment of Cable TV and the address was still visible. It's a house in Inglewood! I got the Firestone Sheriff Department Detectives sitting on the house now, and the judge just granted us the search warrant so we're about to go hit it, and I thought that you might want to come?"

"Of course, Detective Cannon, good police work!" Detective Harris said as he ran to put on his coat and put the copies in a legal envelope as they hurried out.

* * * *

Julian and the girls were all posted up in three different cars watching the pool hall, and dressed for the occasion. Julian was posted in the back of the pool hall in the alley entrance with Gwen, and Lady G, Tish, and Little Momma was at the other end of the alley in another car posted, and princess was with Dee Dee out front down the street posted in another car. They all had on bullet proof vests and was dressed in black with wigs and hats on. Julian even had on a dread-lock wig and a black bandana on his neck to cover up his mouth. They had their walkie-talkie all turned to the same channel and was patiently waiting for Carl to arrive. It was 8:00p.m., at night and only the street lights and lights from the building laminated the scene. It was Friday night so the pool hall was packed with Carl's crew. Niggas was dress to impress and flossing their fliest whips and best jewelry.

Carl pulled up with a two car caravan trailing him. His body guards opened up the back door to his new 500 SEL Benz as Carl stepped out in a nice egg shell white linen suit with some dark brown gator boots and a dark brown handkerchief, with his big diamonds glistening in the light.

"I see that he comes dressed for his funeral." Lady G said as Tish and Little Momma laughed at the joke.

Five more niggas exited the two cars that came with him. Julian held up his walkie-talkie and said, "It's time ya'll let the games begin!" Then Julian looked over at Gwen and said, "Vengeance is our baby." Then she leaned over and kissed him as he smiled and speeded off toward Carl and his crew. Lady G was coming down the other end of the alley, as they pulled up in the back of the pool hall where Carl and his crew was standing and kickin' game to one another.

Carl looked up as the red Malibu hit the parking lot and seen two mask-men jump out with guns, then another old 68 Buick hit the parking lot right after and three more mask-men jumped out.

"It's a hit...!" Carl yelled as he dove on side of his Benz and bullets started shooting in all directions. Julian had a M16 rifle and he shot toward Carl as Carl dove, and he missed and hit Carl's little buff body guard, and knock him back four feet as he painted the back wall with his blood. Gwen had her 9mm and she shot one of the crew members as he tried to run away. Lady G jumped out of the Buick with her modified 12 gauge shot gun and caught one of the niggas who started shooting at Julian and shot half of his face off. Little Tish jumped out with two 45 automatics and her and Little Momma started running up on Carl's crew shooting as if they didn't care about getting shot. Julian and Lady G seen this and followed suit as Carl's crew got up off the ground and around the cars, and started shooting blindly as they tried to run away and get away from their attackers. But Julian and the girls had no mercy and was shooting them down as they ran. Carl's big body guard jumped up screaming as he shot his 9mm blindly at his attacker's and Tish and Little Momma ate him up as they both stood side by side and unloaded their clips into his face and body. Blood shot all over Carl's new off white suit, as he looked up and seen Lady G and Julian standing over him.

"You knew that we was coming nigga! Lady G send this bitch ass nigga to hell."

"My pleasure," Lady G said as she stood over Carl with her 12 gauge shot gun and unloaded her last three shells into is face, erasing all identity from his face.

Princess and Dee Dee pulled up to the front entrance of the pool hall and ran in with ski masks, on and started shooting every nigga insight. Princess had two Glock 9mm and Dee Dee had a Box Uzi and they had only one thing on their minds, 'to put in some work.' Ed the bartender grabbed his 12 gauge shot gun from behind the counter and when he looked back up, Princess had one of her Glocks aimed right at him and Ed seen her smile as he dropped the 12 gauge, and Princess shook her head and shot him four times in the upper body. Princess looked at Dee Dee as Dee Dee was putting in another clip and they heard three loud shots from the back and Princess said, "Come on," as they ran through the pool hall to the back door stepping over people who was laying on the floor. When Princess opened the back door, she was looking down Little Momma's 9mm Ruger. They smiled as Princess and Dee Dee walked out into the parking lot and seen all of the dead bodies.

"We got company ya'll..!" Gwen announced as the police was coming down the alley. Julian ran over and started shooting at the police car as the M16 rifle ate the windshield and body of the police car up.

"Let's get the fuck out of here ya'll..!" Julian yelled as they all ran and jumped in their cars. Princess just jumped in the Buick with Lady G, Tish, and little Momma. Dee Dee jumped in the car with Julian and Gwen. Princess punched out, and Julian backed out to follow Princess and the police who was in the passenger seat of the police car that Julian shot up started unloading his Glock into the back window of the Malibu as Julian sped off. Julian and Dee Dee duck down low as the gun shots ate away at the back window of the car. Julian turned off onto the residential street then looked up in the rear view mirror and said, "Are ya'll a'ight?"

"I'm good," Dee Dee said then they looked over at Gwen and she was leaned over with her head on the passenger window and blood running out of a hole in her head. "Gwen, Gwen ...!" Julian yelled as he lifted her head up and seen her eyes was open but her soul was gone.

"Gwen, Gwen, wake up baby, wake up!" Dee Dee yelled as she was grabbing her head trying to slap her to wake her up. Julian was driving but got distracted watching Dee Dee as a police car seen him coming down the street while they set at a stop sign, then the police car punched it as the Malibu was speeding by and ran into the side of the Malibu spinning it around and into a park car. Julian was still conscious and looking out of his front windshield at the police car that was directly in front of him. Julian jumped out of the Malibu on rubber legs as he grabbed his M16 rifle and went to work. Julian shot a quick round of bullets into the police side passenger window. The police on the passenger side of the police car ducked down as Julian started shooting and the police who was driving got hit in the face as the M16 bullets knocked his brains out. Julian went to reload as the other police came up shooting hitting Julian twice in the bullet proof vest knocking him down to the ground. The police jumped out and ran over to finish Julian off, and caught a glimpse of a shadow in the car and when he looked up, Dee Dee unloaded her Box Uzi all into his face and body, as he fell to the ground shaking. Julian struggled to get up and put his new clip into his M16 rifle, then jumped back into the Malibu and started it back up and burned rubber down the street, as two police cars was coming up fast behind him. Julian hit the corner and when the police hit the corner behind them Dee Dee started shooting her Uzi out of the back window.

"J., where are you? J., where are you at?"

"That's princess over the walkie-talkie," Julian said as he looked around for the walkie-talkie and spotted it in Gwen's lap. He grabbed it and said, "Meet us at the house! I repeat, meet us at the house."

The police started shooting as Julian was talking and Dee Dee let out a slight scream as the bullets ricocheted through the interior of the car.

Princess and them heard the gun shots and she said, "J., where are ya'll at, let us come and get you..!"

Julian looked back at Dee Dee and said, "Strap up baby, it's time to show these muthafuckas who we are."

Dee Dee smiled and started reloading her Uzi and grabbed Gwen's 9mm and extra clips then leaned over and kissed Julian and said, "I love you Daddy."

"I love you too Dee Dee! If you can make it to the safe house, then you make a run for it! You hear me?"

"Yes Baby I hear you."

"Where are you J.,?" Lady G voice came over the walkie-talkie.

"Hey Baby, take care of the family! And keep it GP 4 Life! Love ya'll."

"J., J., wait we'll come and help you where are you?"

"Go home, that's and order!"

"Don't do this J..!"

"Hi Sis, Gwen's already gone and we're gonna ride for her. We love ya'll, watch over each other bye. Watch out J..!"

Dee Dee dropped the walkie-talkie as Julian swerved as the policed car tried to run into him, and the Malibu jumped on the curve then jumped back off as Julian skidded to a stop, and three police car swerved and stop in front of him and one skidded in back of him. Julian jumped out with the M16 rifle and started bussin at the police cars in front of him, then turned and shot at the one in back of him. Dee Dee jumped out with her Uzi in one hand and Gwen's 9mm in the other, and started shooting at the police cars in front of them running full speed toward the police cars with both of her guns sparking. Julian turned and yelled, "Noooo," and he shot one police that was shooting at Dee Dee and Dee Dee shot two more as the other policemen opened fired on her, making her stagger wildly as the bullets ricocheted off of her bullet proof vest then her head jerked back as she fell to the ground.

"Bitch ass muthafuckas!" Julian yelled as he ran toward the police car that was in back of him unloading his M16 rifle clip into the police car as the police tried to hide behind his car door, then took off trying to run as the bullets started going through the car door stinging his body. The police fell down before he made it to the back of the car and Julian grabbed his 357 Magnum and shot the police five times then jumped in the police car as another police car skidded to a stop right next to Julian, and the police shot through his window as Julian smash on the gas peddle and the police car spun out in reverse, and ran over the dead policemen's body as the door slammed closed. Julian swerved and spun the car around, then stumped on the gas peddle and shot off in the opposite direction as the policemen was in the middle of the street shooting at the stolen police car. The back window shattered as bullet raddled through the police car and one skinned the side of Julian's head as blood ran down his face and neck. He felt the side of his arm, shoulder, and hip numb, and knew that he was hit bad as he grabbed his M16 rifle and pulled the clip out, then struggled to get another one in as he pulled back the lever and seen the ghetto bird over top of him and knew that it was over, so he turned onto the main street and stopped. Then as he got out shooting at the police car coming toward him eating up the windshield with bullets and causing the police car to swerve and wreck. Julian laughed and said, "Come on bitch," and put in another clip as a police car came from in back of him and ran him over as he stood in the middle of the street. Julian never seen it coming, as the car hit him and he flew 15 feet in the air and landed twisted on the hood of a car that an old man and lady was driving. The police ran up with their guns drawn and snatched him off the hood of the car and shot him twice in the head.

The officer got on his walkie-talkie and said, "Situation is under control, suspect is down!"

The dispatcher came back over the air and said, "Officer, can you repeat the condition of the suspect?"

"Suspect is D.O.A., I repeat; suspect is D.O.A!"

"Copy!"

Lady G and the girls was in Julian Blazer driving around trying to find the location that Julian was at as he fled from the police. They saw a helicopter flying over an area and drove toward that area as they picked up the police frequency over the walkie-talkie and started crying when they heard the police say that Julian was D.O.A, Lady G made it to the scene where Julian was, and seen his body yellow taped off laying twisted on the ground. Princess clenched her Barretta as Lady G looked over at her and said, "It's nothing we can do," and turned down the street headed toward the area that Gwen and Dee Dee was at. They rode by and seen the yellow tape and white sheet covering the bodies, as the police directed the on coming cars down a residential street away from the scene. They drove in silence as tears ran down their cheeks. Lady G went to the stash house and the girls mourned the lost of their love ones and cried themselves to sleep.

* * * *

After the police gained entrance into Big Bro house in Inglewood they found large sums of money and a closet full of guns. His truck was in the garage with his surveillance equipment and it all was confiscated. Big Bro was very neat and organized so there wasn't much incrimination evidence around that can link him to any organization, gangs, or terrorist group. Everything in the house was confiscated and finger prints were taken. Detective Harris found a photo of Big Bro with his military unit, and seen Latoya Deazee among them, so he pocketed the photo.

"Detective Cannon, if you find anything else that you think might help in this investigation, then call me!"

"Will do Sir." Detective Cannon said as Detective Harris walked out. Detective Harris sat in his car for a moment then looked at the legal envelope with the copies in it and drove off headed to Scott's Deli.

Chapter 11
Mourn You Till We Join You

Lady G and the girls made in back to the Mansion the following evening, and they all went into the bedroom with G-Fly and had a meeting as they all stared at G-Fly and voiced their opinion.

"Listen ladies, it's real hot around here right now, and we don't know how much stuff the police know about us. They got photos of us wearing disguises, this I know for sure. But I don't know how well they could put the pieces together. Personally, I believe that I'm their number one suspect! But they can't put me at none of the shooting, so it's their word against mine. However, they probably won't be coming to talk when they catch up to me, so I'm not trying to do no talking either. This is war, and I plan on holding court in the streets, like Julian, Ty, Dee Dee, and Gwen. We live by certain rules and we ride and die by certain rules. Now peep, I'm gonna give each one of you a million a piece in your overseas bank account, so you can go anywhere you want and live like a queen." Lady G stated.

"Where are you gonna go?" Princess asked.

"Well I'm gonna kill that crooked cop first, then I'll find some where nice to kick it at." Lady G expressed.

"Well, I'm not leaving until it's over either, and where-ever you go, then I'm going too!" Princess stated.

"Me either." Said Little Tish.

"Well we better go find his punk ass then, because I'm not leaving either until it's over." Little Momma said with a cute smile, and her and Little Tish gave each other high-five.

"You bitches is gonna drive me crazy!" Lady G uttered in a joking manner.

"Bitch you were already crazy when we met you." Princess joked as everyone laughed.

"Listen ya'll, this muthafucka family is dead too!" Little Mamma expressed.

"Yeah, so what!" Princess stated with an annoying look on her face.

"Well, they got to have a funeral for them soon, and that's the way we can catch him slipping and get trace on him."

"Girl your brilliant!" Lady G said as she gave Little Tish a high-five.

"Yeah that's a good idea! If you want, I can pick him off with my sniper rifle?"

"No that's to good for him. I want to look in his eyes as I kill his bitch ass!" Lady G expressed as she stared at G-Fly laying in the bed with tubs running all through him.

"I feel you sis, but let's do it right so we can make that vacation and live a little bit longer." Little Tish said as everyone shook their heads in agreement.

"Don't worry sis, I won't do nothing to jeopardize our lives. Julian told me to watch over our family, and I will honor my position in life. So don't worry, we'll plan our moves out to the fullest. Now, let me go make some phone calls and see if we can find out when and where this funeral will be taking place." Lady G smiled as she got up and walked away.

Princess looked over at G-Fly and said, "Daddy you need to wake up, because this bitch is going crazy!" And they all shared a good laugh.

* * * *

Julian mother was all tears when she heard the news, but the secret overseas back account that Julian set up for her with 3 million dollars in it, made her look at his situation in a different light. She knew that Julian was in the game, but the reality of him dying in it never registered in her mind. But now she knew that he was in very deep. Lady G explained to her the war that they had with the crooked cops and why, and Julian mother was furious and devastated. She promised to keep the knowledge and information that she had about the family a secret, and Lady G gave her an extra two hundred thousand dollars for the funerals and the Attorney Ron Johnson information so she can have for when the police tries to pressure her. She promised to give Gwen and Dee Dee a proper burial too, and made Lady G promise to avenge her son's death. Lady G promised and they hugged and parted.

* * * *

Joe was going over all of the information that Detective Harris gave him. He knew that Latoya Deazee was the suspect that tried to kill him at the hospital. Even though she had a clever disguise on, her eyes was something she didn't hide, and her innocent eyes was those of a cold hearted killer. Now where can he find them at was the question. Joe needed answers and only one person could give it to him. He picked up the phone and called Carl's Pool Hall.

"Hello..!"

"Yeah, let me speak to Carl." Joe uttered to the strange sounding voice on the other end.

"Who's calling?"

"Tell him Joe!"

"Joe who?" The man on the other line asked.

Joe realize that the man on the other end of the phone was a white man, and it was no way a white man should be answering the phone in a black pool hall, unless Carl got busted.

"Hello, Joe who?" The man asked again.

"This is his attorney, can I speak to him please?" Joe used his best proper white voice.

"Well Sir., this is Oakland Police Department and I don't think that your client would be in need of your services no more. He got murdered yesterday.

"What happened?"

"Well it seems like your client had made some enemies, we manage to track down three suspects, two women and a man, and after an intense shoot out we was able to subdue the situation."

"Was you able to detain them?"

"No Sir., they didn't make it! It's all over the news, you didn't see it?"

"No, I didn't..!"

"What did you say your name was again?"

Joe hung up the phone and went to cut on the TV, and the news was showing the crime scene of the Pool Hall with the area yellow taped off, and at the bottom of the TV it read; 17 dead and 12 shot in fatal shoot out. Then the news showed both the scenes of Gwen and Dee Dee on one side of the screen then Julian on the other, and at the bottom of the screen it read; 3 shooting suspects dead in fatal shoot out.... 8 police was killed by suspects, and 10 critically injured. Then they showed the DMV photos of Gwen, Dee Dee, and Julian.

"Well I'll be damn, that's them! They went to kill Carl, Gust must've told them everything. That's how they knew about me and Fred. Son-of-a-bitch! Gust got my family and Fred killed. But who are they and where are the other bitches at?" Joe whispered to himself as he ponder the thought. Then he wrote down the suspects name and picked up the phone.

"Hey Scott! I need another favor from you!"

"What can I do for you Joe?"

"I need you to run these names through the NCIC for me and pull up a credit report for me too."

"Will do, and keep up the good work! Scott said as he laughed and said, "Call me back in a couple of hours."

"Gotcha!" Joe said as he hung up the phone then looked at his big 44 Magnum laying on the table in front of him.

* * * *

Princess, Tish and Little Momma was watching the news with teary eyes as they seen the crime scene of their family members. "We should've got out and shot all of them bitch ass police!" Little Tish said in a hostile voice.

"Then we would be able to get revenge on the muthafuckin crooked police who started this whole shit." Lady G said as she was walking in the living-room and over heard Tish's comment. We got the location and time of the funeral, so now we need to go get some G-rides and come up with a plan. It's tomorrow at 1:00p.m., so we don't have much time, and we got to do this right, so let's go check out the area and go get some G-rides and our disguises.

The girls all got up with no hesitation and went to get dress. Lady G looked at the TV at the scene of Carl's Pool Hall and said, "It's not over yet!" Then went to go check on G-Fly so she could gather her thoughts and feed her inner rage.

* * * *

Later on that day Joe went to go meet Detective Harris at Scott's Deli. When he walked into the deli

Detective Harris was waiting at the table. Scott walked over with Joe and said, "Ya'll follow me to the back office so you guys can have some privacy."

"Thank you Scott." Joe uttered as they followed Scott to his back office.

"Scott said take as long as you need!" Then he smiled and patted Joe on his shoulder as he walked out.

"Well, I see that you been busy Joe."

"Just doing what I was trained to do."

"Well I'm curious, was the drug dealer in Oakland who owned the Pool Hall Steve Price's confidential informant?"

"I believe so!" And Gust's family was tortured for this information and the information on Fred and you!"

"Yes, that's the same analysis that I came up with." Joe said as he bent the truth. He knew that he had to put the weight on Steve Price, to save his ass and keep Mike on his team.

"Well, it kind of makes sense know! I ran them names and they came up clean. Also, I ran a credit check and the male suspect name came up as the owner of a social dance entertainment company."

"Social dance Entertainment Company, what is that?" Joe asked.

"It's a short term for a call girl service."

"He's a pimp?"

"I guess you can say that. Here's the information on it. But that isn't the best part!" {Joe's eyes got big as he looked up at Mike.}

"That was his alias name! His real name is Julian Banton! And get this…he's only 18 years old. His mother name is Evett Walker and she just claimed the bodies and is on her way up to Oakland now with her attorney to fill out the proper paper work and guess what else?"

"What?"

"Her attorney is Ron Johnson! Ring a bell? The same Ron Johnson that represents Toni Davis, the lady who Mansion door ya'll kicked in and killed her kids, cousin, and put her husband in a comma. The same lady who escaped from the hospital under police protection and who's babies father who was in a comma got kidnapped from the hospital on the same day. Joe this case really stinks. No, it reeks of foul play! I can't put the pieces together right now, but what-ever is going on you better fix it, or hope that it don't come back and bit you in the ass."

"Mike, I'm just doing my job and trying to catch the sorry muthafuckas who killed my family and my partners.

I'm sure that you'll be doing the same thing if you were in my shoes."

"Maybe! However, here is Julian's mother address. We don't have enough evidence to get a search warrant to search her premises, but being that you're not functioning as an officer of that law, I thought maybe you can use it."

"Thank you Mike, I owe you big time for this! More then you can imagine, but make sure you burn all evidence of this. I'm not trying to get caught up in the shit your in, because no telling were it's gonna end." {Joe looked at Mike with a curious expression.} Oh yeah, some Asian dope dealers got killed in Garden Grove, we suspect it was a drug deal gone bad, but the crazy this is, we recovered over $300,000 dollars out of the bedroom closet. I guess that the other suspects fled without checking the premises for the money, unless they were content with what they got? No telling, but be careful out there and watch your back!" Detective Mike Harris said as he smiled and turned and walked out.

"Joe was sweating bullets and confused as hell as to Mike's motives and intention. But he was glad that Mike wasn't trying to arrest him on any charges, because it seem like Mike knew enough to put him away for life. Joe questioned maybe he might got to kill Mike later on, then smiled and walked out with the big legal envelope.

* * * *

"Hello!"

"Hey Princess, what's good beautiful? I need to talk to you." Killa said over the phone as Princess picked up.

"Who is this?"

"This is Killa!"

"Oh what's up Killa, we've been real busy lately and the flower shop has been close for renovation." Princess spoke in code letting Killa know that they wasn't selling anything.

"Yeah I know, J., told me the other day, and gave me the car and told me to bring it to you after I finish with the sound system." Killa shot back at her in code letting her know that Julian gave him some work to sell and to contact her when the finished.

"O'kay, where are you at now?"

"I'm at the shop."

"O'kay, I'm on my way!" Princess said as she looked over at Lady G and said, "Julian must've gave Killa some work to sell a couple of days ago, because he just called me and said that he had the money. He's at his Rim shop waiting for us.

"Well let's go see what he got!"

"Can you trust him?" Little Momma said from the back seat of Lady G's Cherokee Jeep.

"Who can we trust in this shit? But that's Ty's older cousin and he always been thorough, so we got to give him the benefit of the doubt. But still, stay on point!" Lady G said as she looked at Little Momma and Little Tish through the rearview mirror.

Lady G circled the block of Killa' Sound System and Rim Shop a couple of times before she pulled into the parking lot. Killa came out of the shop greeting them with a big smile. "What's up ladies?"

"You tell us?" Princess said.

"Nothing just getting this paper! Young J., told me to contact you when I was finished. What he didn't tell you yet?" Killa asked.

"No he must've forgot to mention it, how much did he give you? Lady G spoke up and asked.

"Well it was 272 birds, I only sold a 150 already, so I got $1,900.000 in the back of that Camero for you. Tell him that I'll be finish with the rest in about a week and an half.

"You must didn't hear!" Lady G said.

"Hear what?"

Lady G looked at Princess then they both looked back at Killa. "Julian got killed a couple of days ago!"

"What! Hell naw, don't tell me this shit. What happened?" Killa said as he wiped his face with his hand.

"Well it was all over the news, the incident in Oakland, you ain't' heard about it?"

"Oh shit, the shoot out with the police that incident?" Killa asked.

Lady G and Princess shook their heads yes! "Muthafucka, ain't this a bitch, them crooked son-of-a-bitches! Julian was just telling me that he was warring with the police over the incident that happened to Ty, G-fly, the kids, and you! Damn my condolence Baby! Somebody got to die for this shit! What's up, I'm in…! Tell me what you need, and me and my little homies is gonna to lay some shit down for you. Damn, that nigga should have told me, and I would've rolled with him. What happened Lady G give it to me raw. Don't bullshit me!"

"Well it's kind of complicated."

"I understand, but how did my little nigga die...fuck all the other personal shit."

Lady G looked at Princess and Princess shrugged her shoulders, then she look back at Little Tish and Little Momma. Little Momma said, "Fuck it, if the nigga want to ride let him ride, it ain't like we can't use him. But nigga, if you get involved then know that you're flirting with death row!" Tish said as they all looked at Killa to see his response.

Listen young tender, I've been flirting with death and sleeping in the devil bed all my life. I'm a muthafuckin triple O G Ramond Crip, I live for this shit. They killed my little cousins, now it's time to pay my respect and loyalty, and blood for blood is all I know!"

"I always liked him." Little Tish humored as everyone smiled.

"Get in!" Lady G said as Little Tish slid over to let Killa get in the Jeep. "As you already know, we've been beefing with the police. This big time dope dealer from Oakland sent a crooked police and his crew at us to rob us and kill us. He wanted to get us out of the way so he could take over our territory. We found out, and went to lay down the nigga in Oakland and his crew. The police showed up, so we got at them, and while we was trying to get away, they caught up with the car that Julian, Gwen, and Dee Dee was in and killed them all, but not before they killed a bunch of police. They went out like gangsters for real."

"Damn that's crazy, Julian told me about the nigga too, and I told him about the nigga's who was down here from Oakland trying to move weight and Julian said that he had bigger fish to fry and told me to handle it for him. So I grabbed my little niggas and we set up a buy for 20 keys from them, and jacked them and laid them down. It was on the news to, it happened on Crenshaw at the Travel Lodge Motel." Killa confessed.

"Damn, we seen that on the news yesterday. Why you didn't tell us earlier, and play like you didn't know about the nigga from Oakland." Princess asked.

"Because, I wanted to see if you were gonna keep it 100% with a nigga. I'm not gonna ride with you if you can't keep it real with a nigga. But, I didn't know that that was my little nigga that the police killed up there."

"Well the police who started this shit is still alive, and we're bout to get at his ass, so if you're trying to ride, then we can use your help, but it's gonna get bloody so if you're not ready for this, then you better leave now!" Princess expressed.

"Shit bitch, I said I'm down so what's up?"

"O'kay, this is what we got planned and Lady G and the girls put Killa up on game as they plotted there move.

* * * *

Joe had broke into Julian's mother three bedroom house in West Los Angeles, and was looking for any and everything that can point him in the right direction of the rest of Julian's gang. As he searched the bedroom closet he pulled down a sports gym bag from the top shelf, and opened it and seen stacks of money in it. He smiled as he clenched the gym bag in his hand, then went over and searched every dresser draw. As he was going through the bottom draw when he seen a Kodak photo envelop and opened it up and found what he was looking for, it' was a photo of someone birthday party held at a club, and everyone was in the VIP posing for the picture. He looked at the pictures hard and notice that Game was front and centered with three other males on side of him, and five ladies in back of them. He recognized all three of the males who was next to Game as Tyquon, the one who got killed during the raid on the mansion,. Xavier, the one who was put in a comma during the raid on the mansion, and Julian, the one who got killed in the shoot-out with the police in Oakland. Also, one of the ladies in the photo was Toni, the lady that lost her two babies' during the raid. And the other ladies got to be the ones who was in disguise during the kidnapping at the hospital, as well as the shoot out at the hospital, and who killed Debbie and his sons. Joe thought to himself as his eyes turned red. Joe took a couple of photos then messed up the house so it would look like a burglary, then left out with the gym bag full of money. Joe headed to his house to count the money. It came up to $124,000 thousand dollars and he smiled at his come up, then jumped in the shower and throw on some nicer clothes as he went to grab a motel room at the Best Western Motel. He made a phone call and Kicked back and sipped on his favorite whisky. He heard a light knock on the door and opened it and there stood a beautiful black bitch that was dark with hazel eyes, and thick in all of the right places.

"Did you request a dancer?" The woman asked.

"I sure did honey, come in, come in! Wow, you look gorgeous!" Joe said.

"Thank you!"

"Would you like a drink?"

"No thank you."

G. Prince

"Well how much do you charge for your dance lessons?" Joe inquired trying not to say the wrong thing.

"Well, I charge $500 hundred dollars for the first hour and $250 dollars for every other hour, and it's a two hour minimum."

"Well, I got $2,000 dollars right here for an hour, but I need the works." And Joe sat the money on the table.

She smiled and said, "You're not a police are you?"

"Hell no baby, I'm just a horny man looking for a good time with no strings attached."

"Well in that case, I think that I can satisfy that urge," and she unbuttoned her dress and pulled it off as Joe eyes was in a trans and his mouth was wide open.

She started dancing in her G-string panties and bra as Joe watched with a lustful look on his face. He never had sex with a black woman before, and also never with a woman who was a beautiful and sexy as this woman. She walked over to him and grabbed his dick through his pants and he almost cummed on himself. She smiled as she pulled off her panties slowly down her legs and took off her bra as her fat 38c titties set up perfect. She walked back over to him and said, "Let me undress you so I can give you something that you'll never forget."

She smiled and started unbuckling his belt and he shook his head to regain his focus, and slapped the mess out of her. "Get off me bitch!"

Egypt the stripper fell to the ground and looked up and said, "Why you do that?"

"Shut up bitch!" Joe yelled as he kicked her in the face, and when she fell back on the carpet, he started socking her in the face then grabbed her and drugged her into the bathroom while she was screaming and he grabbed her arm and broke it. She hollered in pain as he socked her again in the eye knocking her to the floor with blood coming out of her eye and nose. "Listen bitch, I'm going to asked you some questions and if you don't answer them, then I'm gonna beat your face up so bad, you won't ever look the same. Now where do Toni Davis live at?"

"I don't know no fuckin Toni Davis." Egypt uttered in between slobs.

"You're a fuckin lie," Joe said as he kicked her in the leg. "She is Games old bitch." Joe said as Egypt eyes gave her away.

"I don't know what you're talking about!" Egypt said as she kicked Joe in the dick and tried to run as Joe fought through the pain and dove on her, and started socking her hard as he knocked her unconscious.

Joe got up and staggered to the motel room table, and took a sip of his whisky as he gathered his thoughts. Two minute later there was a knock on the door. "Who is it?" Joe said as he peeped out of the curtain.

"I'm Don, I'm here to check on my friend Egypt that's in there."

"Oh yeah, just a minute." Joe tucked in his shirt and fixed his hair then cracked the door.

And a big black man 6'4" 330 lbs., was standing there in a Fila jogging suit. "Well, she's in the shower right now, I'll tell her to check up with you when she gets finished." Joe said as the man shook his head.

"Nope, that's not how this works. The big man pushed the door open and walked in the room. He looked at Joe and seen blood on is shirt, and grabbed Joe without any warning and socked Joe twice in the face causing Joe to fall back against the wall in a daze, and Joe came up with his 44 magnum in hand and shot the big man in the shoulder causing the big guy to fall back on the floor screaming. Joe kicked his in the nuts as he curled up, then grabbed the bottle of Whisky and started slipping the big man in the face with it. He heard a loud scream as he seen Egypt standing there naked and beaten badly and he grabbed his stuff and looked over at Egypt and said, "you tell Toni Davis that I'm gonna kill them all when I catch them." Joe heard police sirens in the distant so he ran out the door, jumped in his car and sped-off. The police car past him up on the opposite side of the street as he caught a glimpse of his swollen eye in the rear view mirror, and laughed to himself as he headed home.

* * * *

Treasure contacted Lady G on her private pager, and put her emergency code in. Lady G looked at the number and looked over at Princess as they were on their way back to the mansion after leaving the safe house to stash the money that Killa gave them, and she said, "It's the emergency code for the escort service." Princess dialed the number then gave the phone to Lady G as she drove on the freeway.

"Hey T., what's good?"

"I don't mean to bother you, but some crazy white muthafucka just beat the mess out of Egypt real bad, I mean broke her arm and her whole face is swollen and unrecognizable. And shot big Ed and beat him in the face with a whisky bottle. The son-of-a-bitch said, to tell you that he was gonna kill you all when he find you!"

"O'kay, where are you?"

"Where at the hospital, but don't trip, I got this! I was just putting you girls up on the latest news."

"Are they gonna be a'ight?"

"Yes, they'll live! Just busted up real bad, but they'll be fine in a few month of so."

"O'kay, give them both 20 g's for me, and tell the girls to stick with only the old clientele that they know. I don't want no new friends!"

"Got you sis, and watch your backs girl!"

"I will…!" Lady G said as they hung up. Treasure is the bottom bitch that runs the escort service now. She's Cubin and beautiful with a bad body, and just as crazy as the rest of the crew.

Lady G explained what happened to the girls, and that only fired them up more. "I can't wait to kill this muthafucka," Princess expressed.

"His ass is on barrowed time, and you better believe that!" Lady G said as she got off the freeway, and looked in her rearview mirror to make sure that nobody wasn't following them, then she turned right headed for their mansion.

Chapter 12

Fuck the Police!

It was a sad day for Joe as he watched with tears running down his face, as they put his wife and two son's caskets in the ground. A lot of police who like Joe came to pay their respects, but a lot stayed away because of the situation he was in. The funeral was over as Detective Mike Harris, Officer Jack Pen and his partner Robert Blue, and Scott from the deli and is long time girl friend Sally, all walked up to Joe and gave him a hug. "Hey Buddy let's go to Scott's deli and have a drink!" Detective Harris said to Joe as they all gave him their support.

"I don't think that I feel up to it!" Joe mumbled.

"Come on Joe, I got some Jack Daniels in the office that I'ma bust open for us," Scott
said.

"And I'll fix you something special to eat, so you can be strong when you catch these animals." Sally said as she rubbed his back.

"Oh, and I spoke to a friend at Internal Affairs and they're not gonna file on you, so you'll be back on the force in about a week so. {Joe eyes got big as he pondered the thought and Mike smiled} So how about that drink?" Mike asked as everyone smiled.

"O'kay, I guess that I can use a couple!" Joe said as they started walking toward the cars.

Joe jumped in the back seat of Scott's brand new 1989 Chevy Dually truck. As they all caravanned to Scott's deli. Scott was in back of Detective Mike Harris undercover cruiser, and Officer Jack Pen was following Scott's truck with his partner Robert Blue with him in his new Thunderbird. Jack stopped by Detective Cannon car and said, "We're headed to Scott's Deli for a couple of drinks, if you want to come."

"O'kay, I'll meet you guys there," she said as Mike smiled and pulled off, and she waved at the caravan as they past her by.

"She is so hot! Damn I want to fuck her!" Officer Robert Blue said as he past her by.

"Dream on stud." Jack pen said as he laughed at his little partner with the big ego.

The caravan got off the freeway onto Slauson Blvd., and made a right hand turn as they drove down Slauson Blve. They drove passed the Slauson Swap Meet and stopped at a red light. Scott was playing his Kenny Roger

CD and talking to Sally as a gray 85 Monte Carlo SS pulled up on side of Scott's truck on the driver side and stopped. Joe glanced over and seen a young black girl behind the steering wheel and recognized her as one of the girls in the photos. "It's a hit!" Joe yelled as he ducked.

Little Tish said, "Now!" And Lady G rose up from the back seat with a double barrels shot gun, and let both barrels go as Scott ducked down just in time as the shot gun went off and blow Sally's whole face off. Tish raised her 45 automatic up at the same time as Lady G shot, and Little Tish started unloading her 45 automatic into the side of the truck as lady G grabbed her Clock 9mm and started shooting up the truck as well. Little Tish seen Detective Harris opening up his driver side door, as she punched it and ran into his car door as he leaned back into his car letting off his 9mm at the Monte Carlo SS as it passed knocking his door off . Little Tish pulled out into the intersection and stop, as she swerved in front of Detective Harris police car blocking him off.

Tish and Lady G pulled up shooting Princess and Little Momma pulled up a car length in back of them, in a 72 Chevy Nova and started shooting up Jack Pen new Thunderbird. Jack said, "Get down!" As he put his car in reverse and burned rubber going backwards. Little

Momma jumped out of the passenger side of the Nova as Princess got out of the drier side, and Little Momma started eating up the front of Jack's Thunderbird with her favorite weapon her AR-15 rifle. The Thunderbird swerved and wrecked into an on coming car 40 yards back. Robert reached over the dash board and started shooting his Beretta 9mm in the direction of Little Momma and Joe started shooting his big 44 magnum over the bed of the truck, as he jumped out of the back door of the Dually. Princess was returning fire at him with the Box Uzi that she used in revenge for her girl Dee Dee's death. The Box Uzi was Dee Dee's favorite gun and Princess was making it known. Detective Harris was shooting at Little Tish and Lady G as Detective Cannon slid to a stop on the opposite side of the street next to Jack's Thunderbird and started shooting her 12 gauge shot gun at Little Momma and Princess. They both turned their guns on her as Little Mamma ran out of bullets and went to reload, and Robert and Jack jumped out of the Thunderbird passenger side door and came up bussin' at Princess and Lady G. Little Mamma ran around to the driver side where Princess was bussin' at Detective Cannon, but Lady G and Little Momma was caught up in a critical cross fire. Scott jumped out of the driver side door and was shooting his

357 magnum at Princess and Little Momma too. Little Momma seen Detective Cannon run around the back of her car, then came up and shot as Princess let out a scream as a few buck-shots hit her while she was reloading her Uzi. Little Momma came up bussin' the AR-15 rifle like a pro as she backed up to where Princess was and said, "are you o'kay?"

"Yeah, that bitch shot me with them damn bee-bees!" She popped in a new clip and shot at Joe and Scott some more.

A police car hit the corner at the intersection and stopped in back of where Little Tish and Lady G was parked blocking off Detective Harris car. The police was in a good position to corner Tish and Lady G between him and Detective Harris, and as soon as he was about to jump out a 69 Pontiac GTO came speeding down the street and ran right in the side of the police car, knocking the police on the driver side across the street as he tumbled across from Little Tish, and Little Tish open fired at him killing him dead. Killa and Little RC jumped out of the GTO and Killa shot the other police that was still laying dazed in the police car in the head twice. Lady G smiled as she jumped up shooting back at Detective Harris as he ducked behind his passenger door. Big Boy speeded up in his 71 Buick

Riviera and tried to run Detective Cannon over, as she drove toward the Thunderbird as the Riviera ran into the back of her car. Officer Robert Blue ran over and grabbed Detective Cannon and drug her behind the Thunderbird as big Boy and Slim C jumped out and started bussin' two 45 automatic and a Tec 9 at the police. Sirens were heard coming from a distant. "Let get the fuck out of here." Little Tish said as she emptied her last clip. She jumped back behind the wheel of the car as Lady G ran and jumped in too and said, "Let's go, come on ya'll..!"

Killa was trying to start the car but it wouldn't start. Little Tish burned rubber and drove over to where Killa's car was stalled at the Lady G said "leave it, come on!"

Little RC ran and jumped in the back seat of the Monte Carlo SS, as Killa jumped out of the GTO and tried to run around to the Monte Carlo SS as another police car swerved 30 yards away from him and stopped, as Killa started unloading his two 9mm into the police car as Little Momma ran over to the police car with her AR-14 rifle and ate up the police that was in it. Princess swoop up and they both jumped into the Chevy Nova as they all pulled off at the same time. Little Tish was driving down Hoover while Princess drove-up Hoover with Little Momma and Killa in the car and Big Boy and Slim C was in back of them in the

Riviera. They both had numerous stash spots in the area, and they all made it to them safely. They pulled into the garages and went inside the house to lay low until the heat die down.

"P., are you there?" Lady G said into the walkie-talkie as Little Tish and Little RC sat listening.

"Yeah G, we chillin'! The guys are at the party too, so we'll holla at you later; out!" Princess said as Lady G and them smiled and then heard the ghetto bird fly through the neighborhood.

"Damn we missed that Muthafucka again Tish!"

"I know, it was too many of them muthafuckas. But it ain't over, we're gonna get his bitch ass for sure!" Little Tish expressed.

"Do ya'll got something to drink in this muthafucka? I'm still pumped up, that shit was like some TV shit. You bitches is gangsta' bitches for real!" Little RC expressed as everyone laughed.

"Yeah we got some Hennessy I know for sure! Little Tish said.

"That will work!"

"And we got a change of clothes for you, so you can take a shower and wash that gun powder residue off of you." Lady G said with a smile.

"Much respect!" Little RC uttered as he grabbed the glass from Little Tish and downed it..!

"Let me bring you the bottle and some weed to relax you."

"Now you're talking." Little RC said as he smiled.

* * * *

Detective Harris got up from the ground and limped over to where Joe was at, leaning over the bed of Scott's truck holding his side as blood dripped from the side of his stomach wound and forearm. Scott was crying on the hood of his truck, as blood leaked from his shoulder. Detective Harris seen Sally in the truck slumped over with her face splattered all over the interior of the truck, and he patted Scott on the back as he said, "You better believe that they're gonna pay for this shit.

"They killed my lady, she never did nothing to nobody!"

"I know, I know, and they're going to hell for this!" Detective Harris said as the looked over at Officer Blue, Officer Pen and Detective Cannon and said, "Are ya'll alright?"

"Well make it," Officer Robert Blue said as Detective Cannon was holding a shirt over his chest and

192

back trying to stop the bleeding as the Paramedics and police cars pulled up and started asking questions and catering to the wounded officers.

The Captain pulled up and got out and walked over to Detective Harris and said, "What happened here Detective?"

Well Sir., we were coming from Lieutenant Joe's family funeral on our way to Mr. Scott's Deli, and was ambushed by several black suspects with high caliber weapons and machine guns. I believe that it was the same female suspects that killed Lieutenant Joe's family, kidnapped the suspect at the hospital, and who tried to kill Lieutenant Joe at the hospital. But they also had some male suspects with them, who resemble gang members. They pulled up on Scott's truck and started shooting. Scott's girlfriend Sally got killed, and a few officers who was with us got shot, but we happen to hold them off. However, the patrol officer pulled up right in the mist of the gun fight, and was taken by surprise as the suspects turned their guns on them and killed them. Fortunately, they ran off when they heard the other police sirens closing in, because we all was really out of ammunition."

"Well I want a full report on my desk within 24 hours Detective Harris!"

"Yes Sir."

"I want this whole area swept for finger prints and witnesses. Check these stores for any surveillance cameras. I want anything and everything."

"Yes Sir!"

"Detective Harris!" The Captain looked back at Mike.

"Yes Sir!"

"Did you get a good look at anyone of the suspects?"

"No Sir, they all had on ski masks and disguises, so it was pretty well planned out!"

The Captain shook his head, then went over to speak with Scott.

Detect Harris walked over to Lieutenant Joe as the paramedics was placing him in the back of the paramedic van and said, "Don't worry, you'll have police protection like the Pope now, and I think that your fight just got a few more loyal recruits. So rest well, we got a big job ahead of us." And Detective Harris nodded as the paramedics shut the van door and was escorted by three police cars with six police who was heavily armed.

Lady G, Little Tish and Little RC took a shower and changed their clothes, then jumped in the other undercover car that was parked at the stash house, and headed to the stash spot that Princess, Killa and the rest of the crew was. They all was happy to see one another and basked in their excitement as they discussed the event of the shoot out among themselves.

"Cuz, I was coming down the street and seen the police car pulled up across from ya'll, and I just stomped on the gas and told Little RC to hold, on as I ran straight into that muthafucka and jumped out and domed that fool."

"Yeah nigga, you looked possessed Cuz! When you said hold on, I said to myself, this nigga then went crazy and closed my eyes as we ran into the side of that muthafucka. Cuz, I thought that you was gonna kill us." And everyone was busting up.

"Shiiit, this nigga here did that same Duke of Hazard shit!" Slim C said as he pointed at Big Boy.

"Man I seen that police bitch bussin at ya'll, and I said fuck it, and tried to run that white bitch over. She dove out of the way just in time, and we jumped out with guns smokin, you know how we ride Cuz! It's crippin for life!" Big Boy expressed.

"Cuz, you peep these crazy bitches? They jumped out acting a fool! I ain't never seen no bitch get down like that.

Ya'll the truth for real…!" Little RC said.

"Listen we appreciate you'll assistance, and ask that this shit stays right here amongst us. This is the type of shit that them white folks put niggas to sleep for, either with a bullet, needle, or chair, take your pick! We know that ya'll represent a gang and all, but this ain't no shit that you talk about to your homeboys, the preacher, nor in your sleep. I trust that you guys is some real and thorough niggas, so you know where I'm coming from. I mean no disrespect for addressing it, but it's best that we get an understanding now, so we will never have a misunderstanding later. Killa, I want you to give each one of them 15 birds a piece. That's a token of our respect and appreciation, from our family to you! So get money, and always keep it 'G'..!"

"Thank you Lady G and we appreciate the love, and if you ever need us again, then holla, our secret is our secret, we hold no conscious, so you ain't got to worry about this incident being spoken again." Slim C said as he stood up and spoke for his homies.

"Good, Killa let me talk to you in private for a minute." Lady G said as her and Killa walked in the kitchen. "Listen, thank you for having our backs. We're stepping away from the game so we're gonna leave you with the rest of that work. That's all you! My family is grateful to you and your homeboys, for watching our backs and riding for the cause. Be careful and watch your back o'kay!"

"Good looking out Lady G, and if you ever need me, then just come and look me up. I'm not hard to find."

"I will." Lady G said as she gave Killa a big hug and said, "It's a clean 79 Cadillac Coup in the driveway for you. I'll have someone to come and strip those hot cars in the garage tomorrow, so don't worry about them. Just go get rid of those guns so ya'll don't get caught up on no fluke shit, and make sure your little homies do the same."

"My word!" Killa expressed.

"Thank you!" Lady G said as they walked back out and Lady G said, "Ladies it's time to go. Let's make it home before it gets too late."

"And the girls got up gave the boys a hug and Lady G said, "Ya'll can stay here tonight if ya'll want too. Help yourself to the food, liquor, and weed, and lock up when you guys leave.

"Thank you Lady G we will! Drive careful girl..!"

"We will bye!"

Lady G and the girls left and headed to the Santa Monica Pier and threw all of the dirty guns that they used in the ocean. Then drove back to the mansion so they could kick back and relax. As they pulled up to the mansion, it was 10:15p.m., and they were surprise to see Doctor Brown's Benz parked in the driveway. Lady G looked at Princess, Little Momma then at Little Tish. They all had the same disturbed look on their faces. G-Fly must've passed away when they were gone. They all jumped out of the car hurried into the mansion, they walked at a fast pace to G-Fly's room. As they entered the room Doctor Brown and the RN Nurse Joann was around G-Fly bed and G-Fly eyes was open as he looked at them and his eyes lit-up.

"G-Fly, G-Fly, he's woke!" Lady G said as they rushed to his bed side.

"Hi Daddy!"

"Hi Baby!" All the girls said as they bent over his bed and kissed him.

G-Fly tried to speak but his words was kind of stutter. Don't try to speak Mr. Xavier it would be a minute before your tongue muscles start to recover its proper movements. He woke up around 8:00p.m., and as soon as I got the call from Nurse Joann, I hurried up over here. I've just pulled the tube out of his mouth and penis 30 minutes ago, and all of his vitals are doing well. I also did a basic conscious awareness test to check his mental perception and faculties, and from what I can tell, his awareness and mental capability is fine. But I do suggest that he have a CAT scan as soon as possible, to make sure that nothing is physically damaged beyond my current observation. Since technology has started to take over, my hands-on skills has become dull." The doctor said to the ladies as he smiled.

"Doctor we can only be grateful for your time and professional assistance. I know that it's hard to work under these conditions, so we thank you for providing us with your services and skills." Lady G expressed.

"I will prescribe some Morphine for him to subdue the pain and relax the body, so he can rest and heal. Nurse Joann can help you with the basic recovery faze. I'll stop by tomorrow to check on him again. Feed him ice to take down the swelling, and feed him jello and apple sauce for the first two days so his digestive system can start slowly functioning right. If you have any problems, call me, and Nurse, make sure that he stays heavily sedated for the first couple of days, and message his muscles, it will help him recover a lot better."

G. Prince

"Thank you doctor," Princess said as she hugged him and walked him to the door. Then came back as Lady G was starting to explain what happened.

"Do you remember anything Baby?"

"Kind of…!" G-Fly whispered.

"Well daddy a lot has happened since you've been away. First of all, you've been in a comma for two weeks. The police kicked in the door to our other home and shot you up." {G-Fly's eyes was wondering back and forth to all the girls as he tried to reflect back to what happened and listen to what Lady G was telling him.} "When they shot you, you was holding little G, and he died in your arms. {G-Fly eyes started to water as all of the girls was wiping their eyes as well.} I ran over to help but this big police picked me up and slammed me on the ground and I had a miscarriage and lost our other baby." {G-Fly's hands tightened up as Lady G and Princess was holding them.} "Ty seen what happened and came out shooting and killed two police men, but the other police opened fired on him and killed him too." {G-Fly closed his eyes as the tears fell from them and rolled down the side of his face.}

"Don't worry Daddy you know that we killed them! We killed everyone of them except one, and we just missed his punk ass today. But we killed his wife and kids and his two partners that he was with, "Princess said as all the girls was shaking their head in agreement.

"Where's Julian?" G-Fly mumbles.

"Well as we started warring with this police, it got real ugly. First Big Bro died as we went at him the first time. But we ended-up missing him but killing his wife and kids. Then we found out that that muthafucka Carl from Oakland sent that crooked police at us, to rob us and kill us so he can take our territory. Se we went up to Oakland to smash him and after we killed him and his crew, the police swooped up and we started getting at them so we could get away. Julian was with Gwen and Dee Dee, and they got into a high speed chase and major shot out with the police. They killed like eight polices and put a lot in critical condition, but they cornered them and ended up killing them."

G-Fly eyes got big as he said, "Julian, Dee Dee and Gwen's dead?" In a hard whispering voice.

"Yes, only we are left over." Princess said.

Little Tish went over and cut up the TV to the News Station and they were talking about the shoot-out as it read at the bottom of the screen; Police ambushed five dead and three injured.

"That's our work daddy." Little Tish said as everyone shook their heads and G-Fly listened as the News lady described what happened.

G-Fly smiled and looked up at his ladies. "Yeah baby, we've been putting in that work, but we keep missing this punk ass police who started all of this shit, and it's getting to hot out there for us. We kidnapped you out of the hospital at gun point. And we help Lady G escape, so you both is like fugitives. I know that they got photos of us in disguises taking ya'll from the hospital, and of Little Momma because she went into the hospital trying to kill that police, but he got away and like 5 police died that day. So if we got pulled over, it might be our last free day on earth.

We don't know what to do!" Princess said as she looked at G-Fly for some sort of guidance.

"Call Hector!" G-Fly said in a harsh whisper.

"Lady G eyes got big!"

"What did he say?" Little Tish asked.

"He said for me to call Hector!"

"What do you want me to tell him Daddy?" Lady G asked.

"Tell him that I just came out of a comma and I'm in trouble and need his help. Tell him to get the house ready for me and my family and come and get us!" G-Fly mumbled the best he could as Lady G held her ear to his mouth.

Joann walked in and handed Little Tish a bowl of ice cubes crushed up and said, "here feed him this, and I'll give you 15 more minutes then he has to get some rest."

"I know that he can't be tired," Little Tish joked as everyone laughed even G-Fly smiled at the joke.

"You heard me, doctor orders! Now feed him some ice, and I'm going to give him his pain killer in a little while so hurry up."

"O'kay Joann, but can you help me with this?" Princess held up her arm and it was wrapped up with a ace bandage.

"What happened?" Joann asked.

"I got shot and I got buck-shots in my arm, hip, and leg." Princess said.

"Girl, I don't know what I'ma do with ya'll...come on and let me see you!" And they walked out as everybody started laughing.

"Let me go make this call o'kay? I'm glad that you didn't leave us baby. We missed you so much." Lady G said as she lend over and kissed him and smiled as she turned and walked out.

"Here Daddy, this will make you feel better. It's been wild and crazy Daddy, but we've been holding it down for you. Killa even put in some work for you. You should've seen it, we was bussin' at them and they were shooting back, and Little Momma had a big AR-14 rifle putting in major work." {and G-Fly looked at Little Momma and she smiled as she held his hand and squeezed it.} "And I had my 45, you know how I get down. Lady G had a double barrel shot gun and blow this police bitch face clean off, and it was going down. Princess had Dee Dee Box Uzi and was letting it loose for our sisters, 'rest in peace.' We tried to kill all of those dirty pigs Daddy. Ain't no one gonna kill one of our family members and get away with it. But what's sad is, we can't even attend our love ones funeral, because we're all fugitives." Little Tish said as G-Fly squeezed their hands.

Chapter 13
Enemies 4 life

The next day Detective Harris, Joe, and Detective Cannon all was in the Captains office with the Captain and the head Prosecutor for the California state prosecutor office Mr. Freeze aka The Ice Man! The Captain said, "I don't care what you have to do! I want these gang members and dope dealers behind bars facing the death penalty, or in a grave before this week is up! I will not allow this kind of rebellion to be played on the streets of my city. The killing of a police officer is the worse crime that one could ever commit, and I want the world to know that this type of behavior will not be tolerated. Now do what you got to do, but put an end to this shit." The Captain slammed his fist on his desk.

"Captain Sir., Lieutenant Joe Adams has a pretty good hunch on who's the main perpetrators is in this case. The suspect is wearing disguises in everyone of the incidents and Joe has uncovered some photos of some individuals that we know is connected to the man Tyquon, who got killed at the mansion after open firing at the police, and killing officer Steve Marshall and Bob Gates, also they're connected to Xavier Smith and Toni Davis, who was kidnapped from the hospital and escaped at gun point."

{Detective Harris threw the two photos that was blown-up to an 11x12 enlargement. The same photos that Joe took from Julian Mother's house.} "as you can tell, it's a vivid spitting image of the ladies who's in the photos of the shoot out at the AM PM gas station, and from the kidnapping at the hospital. But we have no concrete evidence to link them to the actual crime. I was thinking that we can put their photos on the News, and say that they are wanted for questioning in connection with certain criminal offenses. We can say if anyone knows them, or see them, then contact the local police department. I'm sure someone knows one of them, or seen them around and would report it."

The Captain looked over at the State Prosecutor and he set the photos back on the desk and said, "if I had to guess, then I'll say that the people in the photos has a remarkable resemblance to the suspect in the photos, and as long as we say that they are only wanted for questioning, then it shouldn't violate any constitutional laws against them."

"Well let get it done, maybe we can get one of them to talk and put an end to this ghetto rebellion that's taking place against our governmental structure."

"Yes Sir..! We'll get right on it Sir." Detective Harris said.

"And Lieutenant Adams!"

"Yes Sir., {Joe looked at the Captain.}

"I'm going to re-instate you. The Internal Affair found you not responsible in their investigation. So here is your badge and gun back, and I expect to see some immediate results."

"Yes Sir., and thank you Sir!" Lieutenant Joe Adams said as he shook everybody hands, then walked out with Detective Harris and Detective Cannon behind him.

* * * *

The front door got kicked in at the mansion, Lady G seen Little Tish get shot in the head by the police man dressed as SWAT Little Mamma ran out in her panties and bra bare foot, shooting her AR-15 rifle killing the two police who was in her view. A third police came from no where and shot Little Mamma twice from the side with a 12 gauge shot gun. Lady G grabbed her 357 magnum off the table and shot two shots at the police that shot Little Momma, hitting him in the throat and head. Then she heard a machine gun firing in the back room, so she ran in the back to see what was going on and a police was shooting G-Fly while he laid helplessly in the bed shaking from the impact. Lady G yelled then looked to her side and seen a police holding a 12 gauge to little G's head, she screamed as the police pulled the trigger and then she woke up, drenched in sweat sitting next to G-Fly in a big Lazy Boy recliner chair, and G-Fly was laying in his bed staring at her with an intense gaze.

"Come here!" G-Fly harshly whispered as he lifted his arm off the bed to reach for her and she went over and laid cuddled against his body. G-Fly felt the sharp pain as she got in the bed next to him, but he fought if off and enjoyed the warmth of her loving embrace.

"Daddy we got to leave here, it's not safe anymore." Lady G spoke as she looked up in his eyes.

"I know baby, well be gone soon. Have everyone pack up, we're going to Mexico. I brought some property their a while back and had a house built on it. It was a surprise."

"For real…!"

G-Fly shook his head yes! "And I brought a house for us in Brazil, it was a secret for your Christmas present. I told little G, and told him to keep it a secret from you right before the incident happen." {G-Fly paused as he reflected back} "He promised me that he wouldn't tell you, even if you tried to bribe him with a puppy." G-Fly smiled as Lady G broke a smile herself as she thought about how she tried to bribe little G with the puppy, to find out what she was getting for her Christmas present.

Lady G kissed him on the cheek and said, "Baby I love you so much, please don't ever leave without me again. I didn't want to live without you, and I told Joann that if I died, then for her to pull the plug on you, so we can be together in the after life."

"I'm glad you didn't die then!" G-Fly uttered as they laughed and he felt a sharp pain as he clenched his teeth through the pain.

Lady G didn't need any CAT Scan to know that her man was alright. His witty sense of humor said it all. "I'll go get you some crush ice and jello so you can get your strength back o'kay?" Lady G said as she got up and walked out with a smile on her face.

Later on that morning at 8:45a.m. Big Frank and three of his most trusted workers showed up and was heavily armed as they arrived. Big Frank was Hector's right hand man and personal enforcer. Hector is the drug Lord from Mexico that G-Fly and them worked for, but Juan is Hector son, who's taking over the drug empire and who's one of G-Fly's loyal comrades for life, because G-Fly put in some major work in for the family that saved Juan from spending the rest of his life in prison. So Juan and G-Fly was best of buddies, but G-Fly also had a direct connection to Hector who was really one of the biggest drug lord in the game. And who had the utmost loyalty and respect for G-Fly, Ty, and Julian. Hector was Game's old friend and connection, and Hector and Game had a very strong bond, so when Game died and left the drug empire with G-Fly, Ty and Julian, then they proved their loyalty and worthiness through their blood, sweat, and thoroughness, and stole Hectors' heart and profound respect.

Big Frank embraced Lady G as he got out of the car, then said something in Spanish as his Mexican worker grabbed their guns and posted up in different areas of the property. Two of them had Tec 9's and the other one had an AK-47. Lady G escorted Big Frank into the house and into the bedroom where G-Fly was laying confined to. Big Frank seen G-Fly and walked over to his side swiftly and said, "Who did this to you my friend?"

G-Fly looked up and said, "The police!" Then looked over at Lady G as Lady G started explaining to Big

Frank in a shattered details as to what happen, and the war that her and the girls been involved in.

"Why you didn't call us? We got soldiers all over the United States who deal with this type of problems. Julian should've called me!" Big Frank said in a frustrated voice.

"They violated our family so we revenge our own." G-Fly said in a calm and intense voice and big frank just shook his head, because he understood the codes that they live and ride by.

"I understand my friend, what do you need from us?"

"We need to leave because it's to hot for us here, we need to get to my house in Mexico so my family will be safe." G-Fly uttered.

"Consider it done my friend, no problem!" Big Frank said as he pulled out his cell phone and started speaking in Spanish as Little Tish gave him her seat next to G-Fly's bed and Princess brung him a cranberry Juice and held one up for G-Fly to drink from a straw.

"O'kay my friend, I made arrangements for your transportation into Mexico, and I've got you a good doctor and a nurse waiting for your arrival, and will be there to assist in your recovery. Your house has been already built as well, so you have nothing to worry about. Now tell me about this crooked cop. We can not leave without saying good bye!" Big Frank said as he gave a scandalous smile as everyone started laughing.

Three hours later everyone was packed up and ready to leave. Princess and Little Tish went to the main stash house and grabbed the $4,500,000 dollars that they had put up in a safe, then they went to their personal stash houses and grabbed the money that they had as well as the money that Dee Dee and Gwen had laying around and it came up to another $3,200,000 dollars they usually launder their money a million at a time, so that's why they had so much laying around, they made it back to the mansion safe and a big RV was sitting in the driveway with a big moving truck. Big Frank's workers were loading the truck up as Lady G and Joann was giving them instructions. Big Frank and Little Momma looked at Lady G and said, "It's all done baby."

"She's good!" Big Frank said as he smile toward Little Momma.

Princess walked back out of the Mansion and said, "G-Fly want ya'll to come and see something!"

And they all walked into the family room where G-Fly was sitting in his wheel chair in front of the Big Screen TV, they looked at the TV and seen that it was on the News Channel, and it had Lady G, Little Tish, and Princess photo all displayed on the screen, and below them it read, allege suspects wanted for questioning - if seen contact local police department or call 1-800-2 SNITCH.

"It's time to go ya'll," Princess said.

"I'll have my workers pack up the rest of your stuff and transport it to your home in Mexico, but we better leave now before we get some unexpected company." Big Frank said as G-Fly shook his head and Lady G started rolling G-Fly out to the RV where Big Frank lifted him up with ease and walked him inside of the big RV. The girls and Joann followed as Big Frank said something in Spanish to his workers as one jumped in Big Franks 850 BMW and followed the RV as they pulled off.

"Frank, what if we get pulled over?" Little Tish asked.

Big Frank smiled and hit a switch on the bar as a secret department opened up, and it revealed a couple of AK-47 rifles, a couple of Mac 11, and 10 different kind of automatic hand guns with extra ammunition for all. "If they don't let us go, then we kill them..!"

Everyone started smiling as Lady G said, "I guess that our Mexican family is just as crazy as our family!" And everybody laughed as Joann gave G-Fly some pain killers and feed him some ice.

"Don't worry Daddy, vengeance is ours," Little Momma said as she gave Little Tish a high five and they smiled as Princess picked up her cell phone.

* * * *

Detective Harris was at his desk when he received the phone call from a witness who seen the suspects and gave the location to where they were living at. Detective Harris hung up the phone and tore a piece of paper with the address of the suspects' location. "Detective Cannon we got a tip from an anonymous suspect who gave us the location of where the suspects live. Is Lieutenant Joe Adams back yet?" He asked the secretary.

"No Sir., he's still visiting his wife and kids at the grave sight." The police secretary answered.

"Well page him and give him this address to the location of the suspects and tell him that we're on it."

"O'kay Sir."

Detective Harris picked up the phone and called SWAT Department and gave them the information, and him and Detective Cannon ran out the office on a mission.

Detective Harris and Detective Cannon was at the location with the SWAT team awaiting Detective Joe Adams arrival. Thirty minutes passed and Joe didn't show so they decided to move in before their cover gets blown. The SWAT leader held up his finger and on three they kicked in the front and back door to the house.

"Clear!"

"Clear in here too!" The other SWAT team officer said.

Detective Harris seen a AR-15 rifle sitting on the couch love seat, and written on the wall over the couch in lip stick was; R 6: 8..! Detective Harris looked at the writing on the wall in a puzzling way. Then seen the SWAT team leader reach for the AR-15 rifle to secure it, and as he grabbed it, Detective Harris said, "Noooo!" And a bomb went off and blow-up everyone in the house and the stash spot went up in flames.

Lieutenant Joe Adams heard the explosion as soon as he hit the block, and seen smoke, fire, debris and body parts fall from the sky. He pulled up to the scene as police was getting off the ground from being knocked down from outside of the explosion. Lieutenant Joe just put his head down on his steering wheel as he recalled that Latoya Deazee was a demolition expert. "I'll get you bitches if it's the last thing I do on this earth! I promise you this." Lieutenant Joe whispered as he got out of the car and started helping the wounded.

* * * *

The RV pulled up to the boarder patrol line to enter into Mexico from California. The police officer walked over to the RV and looked in as he seen Big Frank in the passenger seat.

"Hey Sinor Big Frank! Good to see you again my friend." The boarder Patrol officer said.

"Hey Tito! I got a Christmas present for you and the guys. This is from our family to you guys." And Big Frank gave the man a yellow envelop with 100 g's in it."

"Gracias Sinor Big Frank, I'll tell the boys that you send your respect"

"O'kay Tito, see you later my friend," Big Frank uttered as the RV drove off.

"I'm gonna like this place." G-Fly said as everyone laughed as Princess and Little Tish lit a joint.

"Put it in the air!" Princess said with a smile.

The End

Ghetto Theory Publishing
2014

Ghetto Games 1 & 2,
they are the hottest urban faction tales written and a
must read for anyone who enjoys the mind twisting
drama of the ghetto street life and passion that feed our
ambitions to struggle against all odds.

This book is rated triple X for the extreme violent contents that has been realistically conveyed through the un-censorships that reflect the true urban struggles, and realities of the ghetto games.

Money, sex, murder, betrayal, drugs, and revenge only spells one thing, "Natural Born Gangster"

.

LOOK FOR *G. PRINCE* LATEST NEW
RELEASES IN BOOK STORES AND FOR
PURCHASE ON
www.ghettotheory.com
AMAZON.COM

FOR ADDITIONAL COPIES OF
RULES OF THE STREET GAME GO TO:

GHETTO THEORY PUBLISHING

Presents

Ghetto Games

Ghetto Games II, "the saga continues."

Am I My Sister's Keeper?

Natural Born gangster

**Rules of the Street Game that Every Hustler
Should Know...!**

www.ingramcontent.com/pod-product-compliance
Lightning Source LLC
Chambersburg PA
CBHW070819120626
46556CB00002B/572